The Shortage

D1519296

A Novel

By

Ben Adducchio

ISBN: 979-8-691917-41-7

Book Cover designed by Krysti Dahlgren

March 2020. New York City

1

It was a short walk home from the bus. Only about five minutes, crossing Woodhaven Boulevard. She had a tough day, because there was so much to do to close up the office. It was made worse because of the lockdown coming. Every business deemed "non essential" had to close due to the virus.

Her feet hurt. She was wearing flats, but still they hurt after a ten hour day. She just wanted to take a nice warm bath in epsom salt and sip some red wine. "Damn," she said to herself out loud. "I'm out. Better go to the store later for three buck chuck."

She started the short walk home after getting off the Q11. The wind was blowing slightly; it felt nice after being in the office and then a crowded bus. She glanced across the street. Something seemed to be moving. Just somebody walking home, she thought. It wasn't, though. Something just seemed strange.

The figure was tall, dark. Looked bloated. Wearing purple, or maybe black. She thought it was a man, but couldn't be sure. Boy, she thought, he was really bloated. Maybe 300 pounds. And he was staring-right at her.

She could see that something was wrong. He seemed to be checking her out, but it was creepier than that. Then, another person appeared. It seemed like out of completely nowhere, another had appeared.

She froze, right there on the street. She felt like a statue. She couldn't move. Their eyes. They seemed to glare right through her. They began to move. They started walking right across the road, not looking either way. Just step. After step.

She closed her eyes. That helped. She could feel her feet again. Her body. Get moving, she thought. Just keep moving! Get home. It's a short walk. Lose these guys.

She started to run home, as fast as she could. It was a short run down Woodhaven, past the Chinese place where she got takeout at least once a week. Past the pharmacy. She took a left when she got to her street. She quickly glanced back. Please don't be there, she thought, but they were. Two of them. And they seemed to be gaining ground on her.

She made a quick right, and stopped to catch her breath. She was breathing heavily, leaning back against her landlord's SUV. Please let it hide me from them, she thought. She listened. The wind was blowing, but nothing else. No sounds at all. She must have lost them. She slowly turned, looking through the back window of the car towards the street. It was then she saw him again, the dark figure. Its eyes were locked on her once more.

She ran to her basement door, hoping to evade this fiend. Get inside, she thought. Just get inside. Lock the door. She fumbled for her key. She crouched low, hiding again behind her landlord's car. He had seen her. He was moving fast.

She leapt back up to get the key in the lock. She hated that basement door, it was a heavy security type piece of shit that seemed to eat her key on more than one occasion. Okay, just do this babe, she thought. Just GET THE HELL INSIDE.

The door finally opened. She ran in, but struggled to close the inside door. What was wrong, she thought. He was there. He had reached her. And he looked

3

absolutely horrifying. His face was ashen; his eyes sunken and gray.

The sound of her scream was muffled when his hands reached her throat. It would be the last thing she would ever feel.

2

A gust of wind outside her bedroom window woke up Janine Gomes. She hardly slept soundly, but lately it had been much worse since attacks became more frequent in the city. Janine sat up in bed, breathing heavily. She stared at her alarm clock. The red lights revealed it was 4:00 am.

"Oh my God," Janine muttered. She could try and struggle to fall back to sleep, or just say the hell with it and get up. She chose the latter. She wanted to get into the office early today to start doing research at the morgue on bite mark attacks. She had been assigned an investigative news story on the recent assaults taking place all over the city.

Janine turned on her old radio on the bookshelf. Her grandfather used to fix radios and TV sets. He'd given her an old AM transistor radio, as his last birthday gift. She loved that radio. When she was little, she could listen to baseball games on it in the summertime. At night, she could pick up stations from as far away as Canada. Years later, she still used it.

There was a public radio station she could pick up in the mornings that covered local news stories. She listened to it every morning to get news tips. It was almost time for its hourly newscast. Janine sat on the bed and looked at the clock to count down the minutes until she could hear it.

"Good morning it's 4:06. I'm William Nakashima." The station was coming in as clear as a bell.

"New York City is reporting its one hundredth case of the virus," the announcer continued. "A nurse traveling from Europe tested positive. State officials say she's 40 years old and quarantining in her home. It's unknown how many people have been exposed. The governor says state officials are attempting to track how many people the nurse came in contact with. Officials will hold a press conference later today..."

The sounds drifted away as Janine got up off the bed and walked to her closet. Janine slowly wrapped herself in her bathrobe and stumbled into the kitchen. She was so sleepy. She switched on the coffee machine and grabbed her mug from the kitchen cabinet. This was the usual routine the last two years, since she started working as a news reporter for the New York Daily Reporter paper. There had been even fewer sleep-filled nights after almost half the staff was laid off about eight months ago. Janine had somehow survived- because she worked so hard. Not to mention, she made so little in salary.

It was too early to grab the morning's print edition, so she scrolled through her phone for any social media updates on the news. Another girl had been killed in Queens, she remembered. She scrolled through all the Twitter handles she usually checked in the mornings. There weren't any updates available. She'd have to call the public information officer at the precinct as soon as she got into the newsroom.

Coffee was ready. She slithered off the chair and filled her mug. She could hear the faint sounds of the radio newscast end. It was replaced by classical music. She opened the kitchen cabinet, picked out a stale cereal she still had from a month ago, and grabbed a bowl. She needed to finish this damn thing before it attracted a mouse. After filling her bowl with soy milk, she got to eating her breakfast.

Janine didn't understand it, but something very strange was going on in the city. It seemed to be tied to the rise in virus cases. As businesses started to close, and cases started to rise, so did the amount of assaults. Furthermore, a large portion of them involved bite marks on people's necks. Not just necks, even. Legs. Arms. A fashion model even had them on his genitals. To say it was messed up would be an understatement.

She was determined to figure out the link between the assaults and the virus. She'd hit the streets, even when the governor said it was dangerous. She'd interviewed cops, business owners, victims, even a homeless man in Washington Heights, who asked for change by the George Washington Bridge every day. The stories never seemed to go anywhere though, beyond just basic news coverage. Something had to break, or she was going to.

"Okay," she said, "time to get moving Jan." She rose from the table, threw the dishes in the kitchen sink, and headed for the shower.

.....

The newsroom was absolutely dead at 6 am. The collateral damage of having a nearly skeleton crew on staff. If news broke overnight, it would take hours for a reporter to actually get their hands on it and start shaking a tree. Janine hated it that hardly anyone was around to cover news. Now, instead of just getting to focus on one solid story a day, she had to cover about three. That meant fewer sources, and more stories born from press releases. It sucked, but that was the way things were headed in the world of journalism.

Janine was 28 years old, still somewhat new out of journalism school. She was born in California, and went to J school in Arizona. Her first job out of school was working for a Phoenix daily where she was a general assignment reporter, mixed in with some cops and courts. She was so excited to start working that she would spend her weekends just hanging out in the newsroom, gabbing with the staff film/music/TV critic and learning the tricks of the trade from the weekend editor. It was bliss.

After five years, Janine got a call from a former professor, who was working in New York. His wife was a senior editor at the New York Daily Reporter and needed to hire a reporter. Would Janine be interested in the job? Hell yes, she told him. It was a huge move, but it meant working as a hard nosed journalist in the top media market in the country. It meant covering stories that might give her a chance to win a Pulitzer. It's what she wanted, to do something that would be absolutely incredible.

So she packed up her car, dropped off her dog to live with her folks in California, and headed east. Now here she was two years down the line-- sitting in an empty newsroom, waiting for a phone call from a source so she could get another story down on ink and into the next day's edition.

Her phone rang. "Daily Reporter newsroom," she answered. "This is Janine."

"Yes, Janine, it's Doug."

Doug Cross managed the morgue at the newspaper. A morgue is a room at a newspaper office filled with old clippings and folders of stories the paper's published for future reference. At the Daily Reporter, the morgue contained two microfilm machines, along with what seemed about eighty filing cabinets filled with clippings, microfilm and old print editions of the paper. Doug couldn't really manage it all that well because he was also working as a part-time editor and weekend reporter.

"Doug, hi. Did you have any luck with my search?"

"Yeah. I found a few articles I think you would be interested in. What time can you come take a look?"

"Be right down."

...

The morgue was dirty. Black mold hung on for dear life to the back walls, and mice had been spotted in a few different places. Janine rarely came down here. A good reporter though uses all the tools available to them, so she knew she should stop by more often. The place just creeped her out.

"Hey Doug," she said.

Doug Cross had a hangdog face, with intersecting lines of wrinkles covering it. He looked older than his 44 years. This was partly because he smoked a pack of cigarettes a day, for the last ten years. So he really looked like he was about 54. The big bald spot on his head didn't help.

"Janine, I found a few articles I thought you would be interested in. How have you been?"

"Fine thanks. What are we looking at?"

"Okay, so about 25 years ago, there was a really bad series of bite mark cases involving the mole people..."

"Mole people?"

Doug looked amazed. "Yeah. You never heard of them?"

"Doug, I have only lived here about two years."

He smiled. Then he cracked his knuckles. "Sorry," he said. "Didn't realize. So the mole people are these mostly homeless people who lived in the subway system tunnels underground. In the 80s, the population was really out of control. Hundreds of people were living down there. Mostly they were homeless. Some of them were just fed up with paying rent and wanted to live off the grid. Lots of drugs. Lots of other weird shit."

Janine frowned. Sounded gross. "Okay," she said. "Go on."

"Well, sometimes a train would break down, and the passengers would have to exit the train and get through the tunnels to reach the surface. You know, instead of just getting out on a platform. Sometimes, the passengers would have to encounter mole people."

"Sounds dangerous."

"Yeah," Doug continued. "Well, there were lots of complaints about people being bit. By the mole people."

"Oh my God."

"Yeah. And most of the people who were bit experienced the same types of injuries these new victims are seeing. Bites in the same places. Many got infected. Some died."

"How many?"

"Not sure. We ran a series of articles back in the mid 80s. I remember one of my former editors wrote the series. Here, I got one of them for you."

He handed her an old newspaper clipping. It was stained yellow like rotten teeth. The date read June 2, 1985. A faded headline said "Bite Mark Victim Dies in Hospital." The byline read Gregory Painter.

"Gregory Painter?" Janine asked.

"Yeah, he was a reporter here for decades. Born in the Bronx, up near Van Cortlandt Park. Knew the city streets by heart. He could always get a source to talk to him. He became an editor when I started working here. He's retired now I think."

"Know how I can get in touch with him?"

"Last I heard he was living in a retirement community type building, on the upper West Side. I think it's called the Pennington, or something like that."

"Thanks Doug. I'll check that out. Mind if I hang a while to read these clips?"

He pointed to a chair and handed her a folder. "Be my guest."

Janine crossed the room and plopped onto a dilapidated chair. The lining and upholstery was falling apart. She started to scan the article when she came upon an interesting passage.

"The largest group of mole people congregate near an abandoned subway station on the upper West side, near 91st street," it said. "They seem to be led by a gaunt white man in his 30s, who doesn't go by any name. The man explained some of his co-habitants only bite people if they show aggression to his mole community."

Very strange. It seemed these freaky New Yorkers had a leader? Sounded like some sort of cult, or maybe a very disturbing religion. The article went on to describe the amount of people who had been bitten in recent months. Nearly 400. A very large number. Bite marks on the neck, mostly. It definitely seemed like a lead worth following.

Janine stood up and carefully placed the clipping in the manila folder Doug had given her. She took a deep breath and closed her eyes. Abandoned subway station. On the upper West Side. And this Painter, the reporter, now lived in the same neighborhood. That would be her next stop.

"All done?"

Doug appeared next to the chair. "Yes, thanks Doug," she said, "this is very interesting."

She smiled a tired smile and headed out. It was time to make some calls. Time to find Gregory Painter.

3

The Pennington was a four story brick building nestled near a riverside park. The Hudson River was a short walk away. It gleamed in the afternoon sun. Janine opened the door to a lobby that left a lot to be desired. The chairs looked decrepit. The walls hadn't been painted in decades, it seemed. A haggard looking female receptionist sat behind a glass window. She must have been around 55, with tired brown eyes hidden behind glasses. Her hair was a frizzy red, and it needed a good wash. Janine approached her.

"Hello, I'm Janine Gomes. Reporter for the New York Daily Reporter newspaper. I called about visiting one of your residents."

"Who is the resident please?"

This woman was all business. A name tag read Heidi.

"Hi Heidi. It's Gregory Painter."

"Painter. What's your name again?"

"Janine Gomes. I should be on a list of visitors approved to see him."

She picked up a file from her desk. She used her finger to move down a list. After about a minute or two, she stopped studying it. "Yes. Wait here please. I will call up and see if he can see you."

"Thanks."

Heidi frowned and wheeled herself over to a large phone. She dialed a number and started whispering into it. Janine glanced around the lobby again. There was an old movie poster on the wall, some Cary Grant film. It was in French, but Janine recognized the co-star. It was North by Northwest. She watched that movie a million times when she was young, with her mom. It was one of her mother's favorites.

"Miss Gomes?"

Heidi's shrill voice brought Janine back from memory lane. Janine turned to face her.

"Yes?"

"You can go up now. Mr. Painter is quite frail, so be gentle with him please."

"Thanks Heidi. What's the room number?"

"320. Elevators over there."

Heidi threw up her hand and waved it in the general direction behind Janine and to the right. Janine walked over to the elevator and pressed the up button. She removed her reporter's notebook from her purse and started glancing at notes she had put together for this meeting. The elevator opened and Janine stepped inside. She had a lot of questions for Painter. Who was the leader of the mole people? Were they tied to the bite mark attacks in the city back then? Where was the abandoned subway station that was their home, and how could she get in there? Too many questions. She hoped she wouldn't wear out Painter too quickly, so she started striking questions off her list. She had to plan this carefully. If she pissed off the source, he would throw her out and not answer anything. A good reporter had to be careful when asking tough or tedious questions to an important source. You have to give them somewhat of a good impression, or they may not ever answer your calls again.

The elevator doors opened on the third floor. Janine turned left but discovered it was the wrong direction. She walked back to the elevator and headed in the other direction. She found room 320 on her left. On the door was a faded beige sign that said "Welcome" in dark letters. A weathered floor mat lie there. It was made of straw and was all ripped. She knocked on the scuffed up front door. No answer. She knocked louder.

"Who is it?"

A gruff voice answered on the other side of the door. It sounded weak, but authoritative.

"Hello, Mr. Painter? It's Janine Gomes from the Daily Reporter. I hope you remember our conversation earlier today?"

"Yes. Just a moment."

Janine heard the door being unlatched and unlocked. It opened and a short white man with light colored glasses and a sweat stained white dress shirt stood there. He had faded white hair and bloodshot eyes.

"Please come in," he said. "I'm Gregory Painter."

He stepped aside and Janine entered. The apartment was small, a studio. It was filled with boxes, containing papers and files. Probably a collection of newspaper clippings, she thought. Maybe copies of all the stories he wrote for the Daily Reporter. Books were thrown everywhere. The bed hadn't been made. It looked like this man hadn't entertained a guest in years.

"Sit down, please, Miss Gomes."

Janine sat in a rocking chair that was propped next to a door. She figured it probably led to the bathroom.

"My apologies miss. I get few visitors. And I usually don't keep the place that tidy when I know I have no one to impress."

"It's okay sir. I greatly appreciate your time. I hope I'm not disturbing you."

"Not at all. I have been following the story in the paper. But I don't think I can be of much help to you."

His voice was very weak, and raspy. Janine had to start asking questions. No more time for small talk.

"Please don't speak if it will make you weak, Mr. Painter. I wanted to explain to you what I'm doing and just ask you a few questions, for background, if that's alright."

"Go ahead."

"I'm writing a series for the Daily Reporter on the bite mark attacks that are happening, and when I looked at previous stories in our morgue, I found several you wrote for the paper back in the 80s. The summer of 85, to be exact. You covered more than two dozen incidents involving mole people biting and attacking New York City subway passengers. Most of the attacks occurred on the Upper West Side."

"Yes. I remember. I'm old but thankfully my memories are still there, Miss Gomes."

Janine smiled. This caused Painter to chuckle and he rubbed his hands together, satisfied he made a beautiful young girl laugh.

"I understand," Janine said. "You seemed to have made a connection to a source that was one of the people down there, living in the tunnels. Do you remember this person? Who it was?"

"I can't reveal a source, miss, even to another journalist."

"I understand, sir, but I'm very anxious to try and speak to someone who may know what's going on. As you know from our coverage, we have seen almost 300 cases of bite mark attacks in the last month in the city. In every borough. Almost all of those people have been hospitalized or passed away from injuries. It's very disturbing. Off the record, my sources at the police department have few leads. But I think mole people may be involved, again, somehow."

"What did the police say about that possibility? If you don't mind me asking."

"It's fine. They deny the mole people even exist."

"They would do that. It makes the city look very bad to acknowledge they have hundreds of homeless people living underground who don't pay taxes and then go on to commit violent acts. In the late 80s, the population was getting out of control. The mayor made it a major initiative to crack down on them. They sent hundreds of cops down there to flush them out. In some cases, people were shot if they didn't leave. Most did, because they were promised affordable housing in Harlem, and Washington Heights. But it didn't happen. They were bused out of the city to keep the homeless numbers under control. But I know a few stayed down there."

"And one of them was this leader you spoke about in your news stories?"

Painter smiled. "My dear," he said, "I told you I won't reveal to you the name of this source."

"I know, I'm sorry."

"My dear, I'm an old man. And I have kept this to myself for many years, but I fear the attacks happening now are from the same ones as before."

"The mole people?"

He shook his head and frowned. "No. Something much worse."

"What?"

Painter paused. He closed his eyes for a few minutes. Janine thought he had fallen asleep. Just as she was about to reach out and touch him, Painter spoke.

"How much do you know about vampires, Miss Gomes?"

4

He could smell it in the air. The blood. The precious blood. It was all around him, and he couldn't escape the lure of it. Inside, he could feel his lusts, his wants, his urges, about to consume him. The need to drink it, to quench a thirst that bellowed inside of him for centuries.

He was a homeless man, hidden behind a ratty shopping cart filled with knick knacks. It was all part of the act. He pushed that cart through every street, every nook he could find, in New York City.

The T subway train was stuck between stops, due to train traffic. It didn't make sense, since so few trains were running during a virus pandemic. But here they were, about four of them, sitting on the train car. The seats were like buckets, in a blood orange color. They must be about 50 years old.

According to the pandemic guidelines, the people on the subway car had to keep six feet apart. They called it social distancing. Even then, the smell of the blood was absolutely intoxicating. For a vampire, to sit amongst humans for a long period of time, and to not drink their blood, was very difficult. It made one feel punch drunk. It was like a contact high. However, he had to pace himself. He didn't have to feed all at once. But if he attacked one and not the others, he would have to kill them all in order to keep his identity safe.

He pretended he was asleep. Finally, a voice bellowed "due to train traffic ahead, we are sitting here. We will be moving in a few minutes. Thank you for your patience. Sorry for the inconvenience."

He wasn't worried at all. He honestly had nowhere to go, but he had to feed soon. He would bring a human to the others so they could taste and drink, but they wouldn't get the best of it. He would drink the most, to keep himself at the peak of his powers. Who would it be?

About ten feet away facing him, was a young woman. She was dressed in the clothes of a nurse; scrubs they were called. Sea coral blue. She looked tired. She was Hispanic, maybe 30 years of age, wearing one of the coverings. The masks, they were called.

On the other side of the car was another homeless person. He could smell the urine; the piss; the excrement that clung to it. He was definitely human, and not another vampire. The smell of the feces gave him away immediately. He had to rule this one out. The blood was tainted, he knew. It would possibly sicken him.

There was one other human in the car with them. A man, dark skin. He wore glasses and had large muscles. He would be an absolute feast. This was his best mark, his best bet to not only nourish him but to bring to the rest of his family. He decided then. This was his prey.

He really didn't feel like killing the others but he would if they didn't leave the train. How much longer would they have to sit here? The subway had become an absolute nightmare for humans. Train speeds were slow. Delays were rampant. But it was very good for the night creatures, the vampires. The ones who wouldn't dare go into the light. They could feed almost at will, as long as they were careful about who they attacked and when they did it. It would be foolish to unleash hell on a crowded train, spraying blood left and right, where you would easily be overtaken by bystanders or even police. And blood left sprayed on a wall was simply wasted food.

He heard a noise. The doors to the subway car opened. Two of them emerged. One very large, one very short. Jairoz was the larger one. The smaller one, Azul. Dressed in black leather, they were bloated. They had eaten! Those dumbfucks. They never listened. Always risking exposure for a quick meal. The older one was listening far too often to the younger one, and it wasn't producing good results. Vampire law states the leader of the clan will kill first, eat first, and then share if a tribe was hunting together. These two broke the law and must be taught a lesson. Immediately. If he didn't keep the clan in line with discipline, it would be chaos, and all the vampires left in the city would be put at risk. This couldn't happen.

"I told you to wait until I brought you a body," the homeless man said.

"We couldn't sire. He wouldn't stop complaining. He..."

"Are you going to let him speak? Speak to me Azul. WHY did you eat when I told you not to?"

"My lord," Azul said, "I haven't tasted human blood in weeks. I am weak. I must--"

"You must?" The homeless man interjected. "What must you do? Must you always be such a nuisance, such a danger to the rest of your family?"

"I'm sorry my lord."

The homeless man snarled. He began to growl in anger. "Azul, you will take the man at the other end of this car, and drink of him."

Azul stared at the homeless human male, who stank of his own excrement. He then turned to his leader. "But sire, he's poisoned."

"You will do as you are told. You will drink of him. You will drain him. And you will remember when you are sick because of him, the sin you have committed. After that, you will then be forgiven."

Azul frowned and hung his head. "Yes sire."

The homeless man raised his head and stared at the larger one. "Jairoz, you will guard the door so that no one will escape. Your punishment will be to clean this car completely when we are done."

"Yes, sire," Jairoz replied.

"I will take the other two," the homeless man said. "We will attack at once, in first formation. Do you understand?"

"Yes, sire." They both answered at once.

Jairoz stood by the door, prepared for his role as lookout. Azul walked down the length of the car, to the seat directly across from the smelly poisoned human. He kept his eye on him as his vampire elder got into position.

The clan leader slowly stood and crept along the car until he stood an equal distance from the nurse and the younger dark skinned human. He raised his arms into the air. The two other vampires stared at him intently.

Finally, the homeless man clenched his fists. It was time.

Azul leapt onto the sickened human. He grabbed his head and forced it to his mouth. The sickened could barely whimper before Azul's teeth were forged into his throat, suckling violently into his veins, draining it of blood, and then drinking from the fountain that began to spew out of his ravaged throat.

As this was happening, the homeless man flew into the air like a fencer making a final thrust. He ripped open the throat of the dark skinned man with one swing of his arm. The nurse turned to see what was happening but it was too late. Before she could scream, the homeless man had grabbed the dark skinned human and flung it on her, knocking her unconscious. The bodies lay helpless; crumpled on the floor.

"We drink," the homeless man whispered. He started to laugh. Slow at first, then his pitch gained strength and speed.

"We drink."

5

Janine sat in the rocking chair, looking stunned. She glared at Painter, before shaking her head and releasing a long sigh.

"Vampires," She said. "Mr. Painter, are you messing around with me?"

"No my dear. Now please answer, what do you know about vampires?"

"Only that they don't exist."

Painter sat back in his chair and put his hands together. He rested them on his lap. He looked into her eyes and gently smiled.

"Humor an old man."

"I know that they are supernatural. They drink blood. They are bats."

"Go on."

Janine was getting frustrated. "Mr. Painter, please, I need your help. Why are you asking me these questions?"

Painter's smile faded. He slowly turned to look out the window. Janine noticed his hands slowly began to shake.

"You must understand Miss Gomes, that this is all off the record, what I'm telling you. None of it must appear in the paper. None of it must be attributed to me. Do you understand? None of it. This is OFF THE RECORD."

Janine was surprised by how visceral the anger was under his collar. "Yes, sir, I understand."

"I have wanted to share this story for many years, to get it off my chest. It haunts me, in my dreams, what I have seen. I'm telling you this because....because I must do it to clear my conscience."

"I see."

Painter rubbed his forehead. He ran his shaking hands through his receding white hair. His eyes looked bloodshot as he spoke.

"I am not sure you truly understand, Miss Gomes. You're so young. You have so much to learn about life. About how far you will go to do your job. Sooner or later you will face the decision to go forward at great risk, or turn back out of fear and for safety." Painter stared at her with his blood red eyes, a tear forming on his cheek. He continued.

"Many years ago, when writing the story about the first attack that happened, it must have been in the summer or fall of 1984. I had a contact I would talk to on the street. She was a woman that begged for change, outside of the grocery store at 92 and Broadway. You know that place?"

"I...I'm not sure. I think so."

"It may not even be there anymore. Anyway, she gave me lots of details about drugs moving in the area. I wrote a lot of stories about the drug trade that was happening. In return, I would buy her food. Give her cash. Keep her in my pocket."

"I understand."

"One night she told me about an assault she had witnessed, in the area. It was in an alley very late at night. A man had been leaving a party, he was a waiter there, or something. He was dressed as a waiter. He was leaving the building when she saw him being jumped by someone or something in black."

"O.K."

"She told me that what she saw was ghastly. Absolutely ghastly."

"I'm a big girl, Mr. Painter."

This caused Painter to laugh. He turned to face her. His hands started shaking even harder.

"I admire your bravery. You have a lot of the qualities that make a good reporter. But it's not a weakness to admit fear. To face it. In fact, it's the difference I have seen between those who are strong and those who are weak."

"What should I be afraid of? A vampire story?"

"What my contact had seen miss was a vampire. It drank blood and ate human flesh. I didn't believe her

29

either; I thought it was just the ravings of a loon. But she told me where he had gone after leaving that alley. It was into an old tunnel on 86th street."

"A tunnel?"

"A subway tunnel. It was a very small crevice, the remains of a station entrance that had been closed many years before. It was the entrance to the 91st street station."

"That's the place mentioned in your stories that I read."

"Yes. The station was abandoned in the 50s, after subway cars were made longer and it wasn't feasible anymore to run a train from 86th or 96th streets into the station."

"So this...vampire...lived in the tunnel?"

"Yes."

"Then it wasn't the mole people?"

Painter grimaced. He seemed to be drained of almost all of his energy.

"That's more complicated. I'm too tired to go on. I'm sorry Miss Gomes. Just know that the attacks came from something that lived in that tunnel. And it was horrifying."

"Please, Mr. Painter, if there's anything else you can tell me that will help, please let me know. People are dying out there. I really want to help."

"I know. I understand. You remind me of another young reporter, all those years ago." Painter smiled again. "Me, of course, Miss Gomes."

Janine smiled. "Then please, tell me everything you know. Off the record, of course."

"Come back tomorrow, Miss Gomes, and I will tell you the rest. Now, let an old man get some of his strength back."

Janine thanked him and stood. She was even more confused than before. As she left the apartment and got on the elevator, she took a look at her reporter's notebook. There were so many questions that hadn't been answered. Was there really a vampire out there? Who was responsible for the attacks back in the 80s? Could that same thing be happening now? And why? Her confusion soon led to frustration as she got off the elevator. Heidi stared at her from her desk.

"Thanks again, see you tomorrow!" Janine roared as she walked out.

The last thing she could see before she left the building was the huge frown forming on Heidi's tired face.

6

"GOMES, WHERE IS YOUR DAMN STORY?"

The screeching voice of Janine's boss and editor ripped through Janine's ear as she listened to his voicemail. Joe Zarga was a grizzled old son of a bitch. He had been an editor at the Daily Reporter for 15 years, and before that a reporter there for another 10. With more than 30 years of journalism experience in New York City, arguably the toughest news market in the country, it made him quite cranky in his old age.

Janine immediately dialed Zarga's number as she stepped onto the street next to the Pennington. Fortunately, she got his voicemail.

"Joe it's Janine. I got your message. Was interviewing a source. I have most of my story written for tomorrow's edition but still need to get a few quotes from someone at the local precinct. I will have it ready for an edit in a few hours. I'm headed to the office right now."

Janine jaywalked to beat a crosswalk light and raced into the 96th street subway station. She swiped her metrocard and walked over to the signs reading "Downtown and Brooklyn." Only two express stops away and she would be close to the office. It would only be about a 15 minute trip, assuming she didn't have to wait long for a train.

Zarga called back as Janine was waiting on the platform. Unfortunately, she would have to wait 10 minutes for a train. Because of the virus pandemic, trains were running far more sparingly.

"Yes, Joe?"

"Gomes, where is your fucking story? I'm trying to help run a failing newspaper, remember? I can't have you gallivanting all over town when we are on a FUCKING NEWS DEADLINE!"

Zarga was in his usual good spirits today.

"I understand Joe. Did you listen to my voicemail?"

"Who has time to do that?"

Janine groaned loudly. The man standing next to her on the platform gave her a confused look and took a few steps in the other direction.

"Joe, I said in the message I need two hours. I'm heading to the office now. Will be there in 20. I just need a comment from my source at the precinct. Will have it ready for an edit in two hours. It's a pretty cut and dry crime story at this point."

"How many sources do you have for it?"

"Right now I have two. A representative from the community watch group and then also the coroner's office. My police contact will give me a third."

"Okay." Zarga seemed to be calming down. "You have two hours."

Janine ended the call. A booming voice rang from overhead. "There is a downtown train heading to

33

South Ferry arriving in five minutes," it said. Only five more minutes. Janine pulled her notebook out from her purse and started looking at the notes again from the Painter interview. Could the old man be right, she thought. Were there vampires actually responsible for the attacks?

She felt as if a pair of eyes were on her from the corner of the subway platform, by the stairs leading down to the tracks. She turned to look. She saw what appeared to be a figure back away into the darkness. She rubbed her eyes and looked again. There was nothing.

"A downtrain train heading to South Ferry is now arriving. Please stand away from the platform edge," the voice of God boomed once again from overhead. Janine did as requested, taking a step back as she prepared to board the train.

7

Joe Zarga's office was a dingy cracker box tucked into a corner on the third floor of the newspaper building. In it you could always find an overflowing waste paper basket. Strewn around the room were old newspapers, some going as far back as 1987. That was the rumor, anyway. Zarga had coke bottle sized glasses and a receding hairline. He crouched behind his desk scanning each day's edition for story ideas, and for spelling errors that had made it through the last line of defense-the editors.

Inside his desk Zarga always kept a bottle of Wild Turkey whiskey, an homage to his favorite journalist, Hunter S. Thompson. When Zarga was young, he read Thompon's book Fear and Loathing on the Campaign Trail 72, a notebook on the 1972 presidential election between Richard Nixon and George McGovern. Zarga always said reading that book made him want to go into the news business.

Janine popped into Zarga's office with her story just as Zarga was about to take the bottle out of his desk. It was nearly 6 pm; Janine had finished the story exactly when she said she would. She was happy with herself. She was getting better with timing. Her copy was getting into Zarga's hands for edits ahead of deadline, more and more. It made her relationship with her editor much better.

"God damnit, here we go," Zarga said as Janine entered.

"It's solid I think Joe. I got a comment from the NYPD. Talked to an officer that works at the precinct near the woman's residence."

Zarga adjusted the glasses on his face. "What did they say?"

"They are increasing patrols in the neighborhood and are opening a new community watch hotline for crime tips."

"That's just standard."

Janine frowned and handed Zarga the copy. Some editors preferred to read the story on the computer, and email back edits. Some liked to edit a story over the telephone with the reporter. Some editors would walk the newsroom, stopping at each reporter's desk to edit with them right there, where the story was written. Joe Zarga did none of those things. He was very old school. He kept rulers and protractors in his office so he could measure story lengths and determine how best to fit a story in the fold of the newspaper. When it came to editing, he marched to his own beat. He liked to edit each and every story with his reporters in HIS office-face to face. He also wasn't happy unless he was holding a hard copy of the writer's story in his hands.

"Gomes, this is a below the fold piece for a story that deserves above the fold coverage."

Zarga meant the story just wasn't above average. It wouldn't be good enough to go on the very top of the next edition-above where the paper folds.

"I understand Joe. I'm working on it. I spoke with a new source today that gave me a great lead."

Zarga adjusted his glasses again. He must have done that a million times a day. He scanned the story. "Then why isn't there any mention of that source here?"

"I'm not ready to put his information into a story. He's also talking completely off the record. So I have a lot of ground work I need to do."

Zarga's face soured even more than it did usually. He rubbed his temples and took off his glasses.

"I don't like hearing that Gomes. You've also got four, no five spelling errors in this story and the damn lead is buried into the third graf."

Janine clenched her teeth. She had gotten the story to Zarga on deadline, but having that many spelling errors wasn't acceptable, even to her. She had to do better at checking her work.

"Sorry Joe. But it's there--the story for now is right there, in regards to that young woman's death in Queens."

"Okay. Get those words fixed and cut this phrase out of your lead." He marked the copy with a red pen and pointed to the phrase he wanted cut. "Then add this here from the third graf. Shoot it to me in a regular email and we can send it to the press."

"Sounds good."

Zarga pulled out the whiskey bottle from his desk, and then a dirty glass. He poured himself a drink and took a large gulp.

"Tell me more about this source when you can, Gomes. I want to hear more."

"Understood. Thanks Joe."

Zarga finished his drink with a second large gulp as Janine turned to leave the office.

8

It was a rainy day, and by the time Janine reached the Pennington she was nearly drenched. Heidi was her usual grumpy self when Janine walked into the building. There were still so many questions she wanted to ask Painter, about his stories. Heidi called up to Painter's room and gestured for Janine to head up. After stepping off the elevator, Janine noticed something strange--Painter's door was open.

Janine knocked hesitantly. No answer. She knocked again, and nothing. What should I do, she thought. She decided to take the risk and go in. As she walked in, she noticed the window was open in the corner of the apartment. It smelled of rotten vegetables. Janine gagged as Painter stepped out of the kitchen. He was wearing another sweat stained shirt, grey slacks and a dirty kitchen apron.

"Hello Miss Gomes. I'm sorry, I didn't hear you knock."

"Are you cooking Mr. Painter?"

"Yes. Vegetarian dish. I'm also throwing out all my rotten food. Is the smell bad?" He laughed and walked over to his chair.

"No, it's fine." Janine joined him and sat in the rocking chair. Painter offered her a glass of water but Janine refused.

"Well Mr. Painter, I have thought a lot about what you said to me yesterday. And I have a few questions I would really like to ask, to follow up."

"Off the record, correct?"

"Yes sir."

Painter crossed his legs slowly and smiled. "Good. Go ahead, miss."

"You mentioned that you had a source on the street you would contact for information. This source told you about an assault she had witnessed. Are you telling me that the perpetrator of this crime was a vampire?"

"Off the record, yes. I came to find out that he was."

"He? You met this person?"

Painter let out a long sigh. Once again, his hands slowly began to tremble. He stepped out of his chair and stood at the window, looking at the busy street below. A few blocks away was the Hudson River. Painter appeared to be staring right through it, as if he could see the aquatic life underneath the surface.

"Miss Gomes, I am very old. And I know that I am near death. What I'm about to tell you I have never told anyone. You must understand that I haven't told ANYONE this story and that it must never be revealed what I say to you."

"I understand, please believe me Mr. Painter. I will never say that you are giving me this information.

Please, trust me." Janine was exhausted from trying to get this man to open up.

Painter stood with his back to Janine. He straightened up his body and held onto the window frame with his right hand. He began to speak.

"My contact told me that she saw this creature attack that man in the alleyway, and carried his body off to a secluded place."

"Where was this place?"

"I went to the location she mentioned, and I found....blood. A very small pool of blood, leading into a crevice behind a wall. I think it was on 86th street, about ten blocks from here. I went to city hall and looked at some old maps of the city. The crevice was what was left of an entrance to a service tunnel that connected the street to a subway station. A station that had been abandoned."

"At 91st street?"

"Yes." He turned to face Janine. "And one night, very late I entered the subway at 86th and walked the track. To what was left of 91st. It was inhabited by a group of seven people."

"Mole people?"

Painter grimaced. "I hated that term. It was coined by the Times, I believe. Anyway, the seven were by definition mole people in that they lived in the

41

tunnels, yes. But they weren't....they weren't human, Miss Gomes."

"Vampires?" Janine could barely get the word out without laughing. This was nonsense.

"I know it sounds silly to you. I do, believe me. I was a doubting Thomas myself. But they....they showed themselves to me. They attacked me, Miss Gomes."

Janine rose. "What are you saying, sir?"

Painter raised his hand. "Don't be afraid, miss. There's no reason to be afraid. I'm no vampire. Just a lonely sick old man." He sat back down in his chair.

"Then what do you mean, they attacked you?"

"They tried to.....bite me, Miss Gomes. But I have anemia, and they could sense that. Not a lot of blood in my veins. I explained to them why I was there."

"Then what happened?"

"A group of them leapt on me. Knocked me down, and pinned me to the tunnel floor. I could smell the rotten stench of their breath." Painter started to sway a little and looked like he was about to collapse. Janine rushed to hold him up.

"Mr. Painter, are you alright?! Let me call a doctor!"

"No, no, I'm fine. I have to get this out. I'm sorry. Please, just a glass of water."

Janine rushed to the kitchen, braving the smell of the bad vegetables stinking up the whole place. She searched through cabinets till she found a blue plastic glass. She filled it with cold water from the tap. When she returned to the living room, Painter had moved to his small couch. He was holding onto his chest and breathing in and out slowly. Janine gave him the glass of water.

"Mr. Painter, please don't go on if you're not feeling alright."

"I said I'm fine miss." He downed the glass in a single gulp, and held it out to Janine. "Some more if you don't mind."

Janine returned to the kitchen and filled the glass. The kitchen was surprisingly very bare--a small stove with four burners, a countertop with white and gold markings. It looked like the equipment hadn't been updated since the 70s. There was nothing on the fridge except what looked like a photo of Painter in the Daily Reporter newsroom from years ago. Janine filled the glass again and returned to Painter. Color was coming back to his face.

"Thank you Miss Gomes," he said.

"You're welcome. Are you sure you're ok?"

"Yes. Now, please sit down again if you don't mind. There's more to tell you."

Janine did as she was told. Painter again took a large gulp from the water glass, but this time he didn't finish it. He licked his lips and closed his eyes again.

"Now," he said, "the rotten smell of their breath--it was disturbing. I was terrified. I knew I was going to die. But then something happened."

Janine raised her eyebrows. "What?"

"Another emerged from the tunnel. It was ghastly. A gaunt man, dressed in purple and black; I remember he wore a very long black robe with a hood. He told them to get off me."

Janine was getting anxious. She started tapping her foot. "This was their leader, I guess?"

"Yes. I couldn't believe it because he was so much weaker looking than they were, but he ruled over them. Told them what to do. He asked me what I was doing there. I explained who I was, again. He said that he knew who I was."

"How is that possible?" Janine's patience was starting to wear out.

"He knew the old woman. She was.....well, she was not like them, but she was strange. The woman had led me to him, because he had wanted my help."

Janine sat back in her chair. Her foot tapping intensified. This was absolutely insane. This man was a seasoned reporter with four decades of experience, who had been nominated years ago for a Pulitzer Prize in investigative reporting. Now, here he was claiming not only that he had met a vampire, but had been working with one as well.

"You helped him?"

"Yes, I did Miss Gomes. He told me that in order to live I had to help him. They wanted food. The city had become overrun with homeless, who took to the subways. The mole people, as you say. They were fighting for territory with this---vampire, and his seven followers, or gang, whatever you want to call them. They needed food."

"But why specifically did they want you?"

"I was the most influential person the old woman knew, and therefore she thought I had the best chance to help them. The old woman was a special human contact the vampires use to survive. They call them---guardians."

"Guardians?"

"Yes, humans who act as assistants to the vampires. They provide them with food, or information, really, about a particular area. This has been the case for centuries."

Janine became absolutely exasperated. She rose and her face became flushed. She was absolutely fed up with this nonsense. People were dying out there, and she didn't have any time to screw around anymore with a nut job.

"Sir," she said, "I don't know if you're saying these things because you're sick, or because you actually believe them, or if you're just screwing with me, but I

45

can't take this anymore. This isn't a comic book. I need answers, and you're really wasting my time!"

She stormed out. She could hear Painter yelling behind her, apologizing and pleading with her to stay. She didn't care. She stomped to the elevator and could barely make out Painter's faded words as the elevator doors closed in on her.

9

Janine stood on the subway platform at 96th street, barely able to control her anger. She was swaying back and forth, and felt like throwing a punch. This was total bullshit. Vampires in New York City? If that were the case, how come they hadn't been exposed in more than 200 years of the city's existence?

She felt again as if a pair of eyes were watching her. Her leg tingled, as if she could sense danger was near. She quickly darted her eyes to the right, toward the far corner of the platform next to the ladder leading down to the tracks. A figure, dressed in black, stood there. She quickly yelled out "HEY!" The figure seemed to fly off the platform and soared into the darkness.

"HEY!" Janine yelled again as the platform bystanders watched in wonder. She couldn't tell if they saw the figure or not. Janine ran toward the corner of the platform.

"HEY ASSHOLE!" She yelled again into the gaping mouth of darkness. Nothing. No one answered. The tunnel faded into light as she saw a train approaching. She tried to look in each corner of the tunnel to see if something was there, on the tracks, but nothing appeared. It definitely WAS NOT her mind playing tricks on her. Something had been there, watching her. Something...or someone. She couldn't explain it, but it felt very real. And very terrifying.

Janine walked over towards the center of the platform. The crowd kept staring at her, wondering if she was crazy.

"I'm just an actress," she said, "running lines for my play."

The train entered the station. She wanted to get on, to go back to the newsroom and work on two stories that needed to be finished before a morning deadline. But she just couldn't. She knew that Painter must have honestly believed what he was telling her, and that even if he probably wasn't right, something was happening that couldn't be explained. She stood on the platform and opened her notebook, examining the notes Painter had given her.

"Hey, put a damn mask on," someone said.

Janine looked up and saw an elderly black woman, probably in her mid 70s, on the platform. She was dressed head to toe in green, wearing plastic gloves and a blue surgical mask. She was obviously saying this because of the virus.

"I'm sorry," Janine replied, "I will have to get one."

"Here, I'm selling them," the woman answered. "Five bucks, I make them myself."

The lady opened a suitcase she had on the platform. Inside were five different surgical masks, with various designs on them. One was beautifully floral, with red and yellow colors covering the mask.

"I'll take the floral one," Janine said. She handed the woman a five dollar bill.

"Nice doing business with you lady. Now put it on, before you make someone sick."

Janine attached it to her face and looked at her notes again. Painter's story was absolutely offbeat, but he definitely seemed to believe it. Following his words in her notebook, she kept thinking about the mole people and the vampire who apparently lived at 91st street. She was standing near 91st street at that very moment, and twice she had felt somewhat of a dark presence there. She still didn't buy what Painter was selling, but she thought it was worth one more conversation with him.

Instead of waiting for another train, Janine started the long walk back up the subway steps to the opening on Broadway. Her phone rang. It was Zarga. The second time he had called today. Undoubtedly he wanted an update on when he could start reading her copy. She could almost feel him shouting down his telephone to leave her a nasty voicemail. But screw him, he could wait.

She had to figure out once and for all if Painter was lying.

10

They had had their fill of blood on the subway, but he knew that they would want more. Their lust for it was insatiable. It had begun, they had started turning on one another to drink it. The virus was contaminating the food supply. So many people in New York City were sick. Too sick to eat. And so many were staying in their homes--away from public spaces. It was called social distancing, and it had put a major hindrance on him and his entire way of life. So the horde had to start eating each other to survive. There were now only the three of them left---along with the Old One, but no one had heard from him in the longest time. He was surely dead after their last meeting. Maybe not, but it didn't really matter.

Azul and Jairoz could be contained. Azul liked to pretend he was in charge; eating before it was necessary, risking exposure so he could feast--but he was always able to be contained. Jairoz was a good soldier, but a mercenary. His loyalty could be bought, so he had to make sure Jairoz would never want to serve another.

He had forgotten his own name. He lived amongst the humans as a homeless man for the longest time, so he just went by Man if it was necessary to give a name. Azul and Jairoz called him lord, but he thought that was silly. It was an old code taught to them by the Old One--a structure, a line of leadership that had to be obeyed. He didn't think of himself as a lord, but he didn't mind it either when Azul and Jairoz called him by that name. It was one of the last things that connected him to the Old One.

He had been turned into a vampire by the Old One. This was years ago, he couldn't remember when. He did recall that the Dodgers were playing in Brooklyn when it happened. He and the Old One would live near the stadium in the warm months, so when games were over it was easy to grab a human. And feast. It was glorious. He would only eat after the Old One had finished. That was also part of the code---the elders eat first, then the young. It was something he wanted to live by, but Azul of course seemed to have other ideas.

He would think of his first days in Brooklyn often. Everything he had learned had been from the Old One. He knew when to leave home, and when it was necessary to return. He knew where to find covering, and when and where it was easiest to avoid light. He didn't want to live in a subway tunnel, deep under the ground; he wanted to live with more class and dignity. He wanted to live amongst the humans as much as he possibly could. And he did--for many years.

"My lord, Azul has left again."

Jairoz had brought him back to the present. No more dreaming. Man snarled his teeth at Jairoz.

"Can't you keep a closer eye on him?"

"I'm sorry my lord. He said he was going to find food for us. We haven't eaten since that trip on the subway. Azul and I were both hungry."

"It is not his job to find food. He doesn't understand what we are even looking for. Come, we must find him."

At the time the virus hit they were living in an abandoned building in northern Manhattan. Years before, it had been an unemployment office. Now it was literally crumbling, with graffiti sprayed all over its outside walls. There was a beautiful park nearby; it was a good place to find food on short notice. But parks were closing, and fewer people were out. So in order to avoid exposure, Man took them to a different location. It was inside a museum. It was inside the park, and it usually attracted hundreds of tourists every week. It contained tapestries, and a roof garden that gave one a good view of what was happening for miles around. Since museums were closed, they could stay inside the museum. No one would bother them, unless they committed a dumb mistake.

And he hoped, at that moment, that Azul hadn't made one.

11

"Oh no, now what the hell do you want?"

Heidi frowned as Janine walked back through the doors to the Pennington. Janine wondered when the last time was that Heidi had had any fun at all. She seemed to be perpetually grumpy, gruff and pissed off. Heidi reminded Janine of one of her grandmother's sisters, whom she had known when she was little.

"Sorry Heidi, I had forgotten something and needed to quickly run outside to make a call. I'm going to need just a little bit more time with him."

"Fine. Just please promise me you won't give me any more trouble today."

Janine was confused. What trouble had she given? It was almost as if the residents here were prisoners who should be kept under lock and key, hidden from the outside world.

"Sorry, Heidi," she said. "I promise I will be out of your hair soon." She really wanted to say your hair that looked frizzy, limp and unwashed, but she decided not to stoop that low.

Janine was surprised to see Painter standing in the hallway as she got off the elevator. He had a smile on his face, although he was trembling. He was holding onto his door frame to support himself.

"Miss Gomes, thank you so much for coming back. Please come inside," he said to her. His voice was even weaker than usual.

"Thank you for letting me come back," Janine replied. She sat in her usual chair and went straight to business. Painter held on to his door a few moments longer as Janine spoke to him.

"Sir, I don't mean to be obstinate. I'm sorry that I was rude to you. But please understand, this story sounds ridiculous." She held up a hand to stop him from answering. "However, I know that you believe it to be true, and I want to give you the benefit of all doubt. I respect you, and what you have done for the newspaper. You were nominated for a Pulitzer. I want to listen to what you have to say."

Painter closed the door slowly. He shuffled over to his chair and sat down.

"Thank you, Miss Gomes. I am very grateful."

"Now Mr. Painter, you were speaking about something called a guardian."

"Yes," Painter replied, "but honestly that isn't as important as the other things I have to tell you."

"Go on then."

"My contact on the street, this woman, knew where these creatures lived. The vampires. It was at the station there at 91st. It had been abandoned for about...30 years at the time. As I said, I went there to find them. They spared my life, because they needed my help. The station had been overrun by homeless people living in the tunnels, so the vampires had to start attacking them to defend their territory. That's how it all began. The bite attacks."

"OK."

"That's what he told me," Painter went on to say. "The attacks were happening because they were feeling threatened."

"This again, was the vampire in charge, who said this to you?"

"I know how it sounds, but yes, Miss Gomes."

Janine could feel the hairs stick up on her arms. "Who was this vampire?"

Painter played with his glasses as he tried to remember. "He didn't have a name. Well, no, that's not true. He did, but they didn't call him by any name that you or I would recognize. He was very thin. I remember that. He was also very tall, almost seven feet tall, if I remember it correctly."

Painter's voice was fading out like a flashlight losing its battery. Janine was getting worried about him again.

"Please, Mr. Painter, don't speak if you are feeling too weak."

"No I must. Please, let me have some water, miss."

Janine got up and went to the kitchen. She turned on the tap and let the cold water run before she filled his glass. She returned to the living room and handed it to him. After a few large gulps, Painter closed his eyes and dropped his head. He cleared his throat and tried speaking again.

"He was their leader, and he needed my help to find food for him."

"But that doesn't make sense. Vampires drink blood don't they? So why didn't they just drink from the mole people?"

Painter cringed when hearing that term again. "You must understand Miss Gomes, that this was during the 80s, when AIDS was running rampant in the city. So was drugs. These people who had set up at the station, they were almost all using heroin, very badly, and some of them did have other diseases. Back then the city was a cesspool of drug abuse. Even Bryant Park, which you probably visit today, was filled with junkies at the time. We called it Needle Park."

"Wow, I had no idea."

"Yes. Some of the people there at 91st had been kicked out of the park. Others just lived in the tunnels because no one really bothered them there. Until they clashed with the vampires." He paused. "Anyway, the creatures needed food. They asked me to collect food for them, which I did. Feral cats, mice, birds. I thought that if I kept them satisfied, they wouldn't bother anyone. It's what their leader really wanted. To be left in peace."

"But they were still attacking people, weren't they?"

"Yes. Some of them were. The leader was trying to stop them, but it wasn't working. He hoped if he had someone finding food for them, that they wouldn't have to go out. That they would be satisfied. But they weren't. And one night, his vampire horde went out and attacked several people. It was horrific. 30 people in the city were killed. My editors at the paper called it the Midnight Massacre in Manhattan."

"Oh my God. But...I didn't come across anything like that when I read your news stories."

"Yes. I should have written the truth, that the city had these creatures, and they were doing all of this carnage. But I didn't. I asked for protection from the leader, and we came to an agreement."

"What do you mean, Mr. Painter?"

"Miss Gomes, I wrote articles in the paper that the mole people had committed the attacks. It was a lie. The midnight massacre became a story about looters and drug users, when it should have been about exposing so much more. The mayor subsequently cracked down on the homeless. He rounded up many of them, and put them on buses, and shipped them out of the city. The police arrested those who wouldn't comply. And I know that some were also killed."

Painter started crying. He put his head in his hands and sobbed.

"I lied to protect myself, Miss Gomes. I lied on behalf of the ghouls. In return, the leader and his followers agreed to leave the city and leave me untouched. I never heard from them again, never saw them again. And the attacks seemed to stop."

"But now they are happening again."

Painter raised his head. His face was covered in tears; his haggard eyes red as blood, showing the age of a man who had been truly beaten and destroyed by life.

"I prayed every night that this would be over. I prayed to Saint Michael, that he would save me from the snares of the devil that I had protected. But now I know...I know that my prayers were in vain. I can't escape the mistakes I have made."

"So the leader then must have come back, since these attacks are happening again?"

"I don't know. I'm too old and weak to find out. But perhaps you can. I know in my heart that they must be behind these incidents. I don't know why they broke our agreement, but I hope you will be able to find out."

"Mr. Painter, it sounds like you're asking me to make contact with these.....things."

Painter stood slowly. He walked back to the window and stared out onto the Hudson River, gleaming brightly in the sun.

"You want to know what is happening, Miss Gomes? Then go to the station at 91st street. I feel that it is where you will find your answer."

"Mr. Painter, it's my job to tell the truth about what is happening. And if what you've just told me is truly correct, then I will need you to go on record. People won't believe this unless someone reliable is speaking to them. ON RECORD. They will want facts, and only you can tell that to them."

Painter turned to face her. He closed his eyes again for what seemed the longest time. "Very well, Miss Gomes. If you are able to find them, and verify that they are doing this harm again, then I will do whatever I can to help you. Good luck."

Janine stood and walked to the door.

"Do you believe in the power of prayer, Miss Gomes?"

Janine turned to face Painter. "No, I can't say that I do sir."

Painter smiled his weak smile at her again. "That's OK. You will, before this is over miss. Trust me, you will."

Painter slowly lowered his head as Janine turned and walked back out the door.

12

"THE COPY GOMES! I NEED TO SEE COPY!"

Zarga's voice bellowed through her cell phone as she listened to her messages. His screaming voicemails were like a broken record, constantly playing on her cell phone over and over. Janine noticed though he sounded even angrier than usual. She knew she still had till morning to meet her deadline, but Joe liked to see first drafts of stories when it was possible.

Janine called him back while waiting for the subway. She got his voicemail. He was probably either in a news meeting or having to battle with the paper's owner and publisher over advertising revenue again. The paper was losing revenue steadily over the last several months, mostly because of the lousy marketing and advertising departments at the paper, who didn't know what the hell they were doing. Zarga was constantly fighting them to keep editorial control of the newspaper. Advertisers wanted positive coverage of their products, or businesses, or industries. Zarga wanted to write good news, and honest news. It was a never ending battle.

Janine put on her mask to make sure no one yelled at her again. As she entered the subway car, it was emptier than usual for this time of day. She wondered if people were just afraid to go out because of the virus. One of her stories that was due the following day was a fluff piece about how restaurateurs were battling the virus by expanding delivery service. The other was a follow up on the woman's death in

Queens. She looked over her notes in her reporter's notebook as the train slugged along the uptown line.

***

The newsroom was buzzing when she arrived at the offices, with reporters hustling and bustling to get stories to press. She usually stayed away from the reporters, unless she was collaborating with someone on an investigative piece. She spent most of her time at the morgue getting background, or at her desk on the phone or typing. Other than Zarga, she hardly interacted with anyone at the paper.

"JANINE! Did you hear about the subway attack?"

It was Beverly, a young Vietnamese woman who had been interning at the paper for the last few months. She helped Janine a lot with background research on her stories. She was also a master at social media and was helping to handle all social media pages for the paper.

"No, what are you talking about?" Janine replied.

"OH MY GOD! Janine, Zarga's been screaming about it for most of the day. There was a brutal attack on the subway, with the victims being bitten! Another bite attack Janine! The M-T-A was refusing to talk about it, but there was a witness apparently who..."

"Take it easy Beverly! Slowly, just tell me slowly, what's going on."

"OK. So someone witnessed an attack, a maintenance worker. Apparently, there was a homeless person attacking people on the T line, downtown."

"When?"

"A few days ago. I don't know how this happened, but we got the scoop! Mr. Zarga and Mr. Rodriguez helped me put a web story together and we have it on social media. Zarga put Ben on the story, because..." Her voice lowered to a whisper so only Janine could hear her. "It was his cousin apparently who witnessed it! He's getting the front page tomorrow."

"Damn. Good for him. Is Joe in his office?"

"I think so. He's been asking about you, going around asking if anyone has seen you today."

"Thanks Bev for the head's up. I'll go see him."

Janine crossed the newsroom and saw that Zarga's office door was closed. He emerged just as Janine was about to knock.

"Get in here," he said. Janine did as she was told. The Wild Turkey bottle was out on his desk, and nearly empty. The office was even more cluttered than usual, with cardboard boxes lying around filled with papers.

"What's all this, Joe?" Janine asked.

"We got some FOIA documents sent to us finally, for Rodriguez. His series on abuse at the state juvenile pen." FOIA was an acronym for the Freedom of Information Act. It was a law that allowed journalists and even regular people to request documents from government agencies.

Ben Rodriguez was a good reporter, one of the people Janine respected the most at the paper. As a writer though, he wasn't very strong. However, Janine did think that he was great at filing FOIA requests, and holding truth to power.

"OK Gomes," Zarga said, "when can I see copy?"

"Joe, why'd you give Rodriguez the subway attack story? Looks like he's already got his hands full with this."

"Because you WEREN'T HERE. I couldn't get you on the phone either, and I needed to get the wheels in motion. We are leading with it tomorrow. We're also doing a special web version, Beverly's helping with it."

"Good, she's great. And I guess he's the next best thing you've got, after me."

That comment broke the ice. Zarga smiled and pulled out his glass from his desk. He emptied the rest of the Wild Turkey in it. He sipped as he asked his next question.

"OK Gomes, when can I see copy?"

"The restaurant piece is pretty much done. I still need one more interview before I finish writing the Queens follow up. But I will have them both for you before the deadline tomorrow."

"Good. Talk to Rodriguez. Let's see if we can connect these two attacks. Maybe there are similarities. I would bet on it. And please do a GODDAMNED BETTER JOB of answering your phone."

"Got it. Anything else?"

"I'm guessing you were working on your source. How's that going? Can we get them on the record in print for this follow up?"

"Right now I'm working them as deep background. But they've agreed to go on record, when the time is right."

Zarga's eyes brightened. He took another sip of the whiskey. "Good, that's very good, Gomes. Keep at it. How soon do you think we can turn them around?"

"I'm just not sure. Ask me that again next week."

Zarga's smile faded. "That long, huh? Doesn't sound too promising."

"I'm working it the best I can, Joe."

"Fine. Get the hell out of here and start writing."

13

Ben Rodriguez came from a Mexican-American family that owned a restaurant in Inwood, West Virginia. It was the only Mexican restaurant in that town, and the only one in all of Berkeley County. Ben grew up in a kitchen, but wanted to be a writer from a very young age. He actually wanted to write food criticism, for Food and Wine Magazine, but his writing skills ended up landing him a job at the Daily Reporter in New York City.

Janine walked over to his desk, where Ben was busy writing a story for the next day's edition. Janine knew that he must be working hard against his deadline. Ben's forehead was covered in sweat and his shirt sleeves were rolled up. He smelled of smoke; he must have been inhaling cigarettes outside all day while trying to get his story done.

"How's the story going?" Janine asked him.

"Oh, hey. It's...it's fine. It's just basic coverage right now. Trying not to put too much blood in the lead, but what happened was nasty."

"Listen, I don't want to bother you. But I have to ask, where were those people on the subway bitten?"

Rodriguez stopped typing. He rummaged through his desk. "Neck, wrists, I think. Let me check my notes." He pulled out his reporter's notebook. He had to flip a few pages to find the answer. "Yeah, that's right."

It fit the description of the Queens killing, but without an examination of the bodies Janine couldn't be sure. Still, it must be connected, she thought. Groups of people weren't just randomly murdered on the subway. It just didn't happen in present day New York.

"Thanks Ben. Good luck with it. Do you have any photos of the bodies?"

"Police aren't sharing that much at the moment. Still waiting to hear back from the NYPD on any motive, or witnesses."

Janine remembered that there was a witness; Beverly had said there was a witness. Ben hadn't shared that with her. He must be playing it close to the chest. Janine's guess was that this witness must have spoken directly to Beverly, or she wouldn't have known about it, either.

"OK. Thanks Ben. Have a good night. If you need any help, give me a ring. I can share with you the autopsy report I got from the Queens killing if you want. Maybe it will help?"

"If you think so, Janine, I will take a look. If you think there's a connection there, I will take a look. Otherwise, to be honest I won't bother with that. I've got this story and a shitload of FOIA documents to sort through. That's going to take weeks. Zarga's breathing down my damn neck. Honestly, that guy is going to have a heart attack if he doesn't watch out. I know he drinks hard, but damn. He doesn't relax, like ever."

Janine laughed. "I know. Ok, will read through it again and send it to you if it looks like there's a similarity."

Janine crossed the newsroom to get to her desk. She turned on her computer and waited for the computer to update. That was frustrating. She took a moment to look across the newsroom. Most everyone had gone home. The place looked like a funeral parlor, it was so dark and gloomy. Other than Rodriguez, who was typing as hard as he could, she couldn't see anyone else. Beverly had left. A light was on under Zarga's door, but his office door was closed. The sports reporters were working at the far end of the newsroom; she could see a few people milling about. Janine thought about the figure she had seen on the subway platform that day, how creepy and disturbing it was. She thought of Painter, in his tiny apartment on the upper West Side, and everything he had told her. She thought of her family back out west. She needed to call them, just to say hey. She missed them. The life of a journalist was very difficult, but not just for her. For anyone who really cared about the job. You couldn't just clock in and then do it half-assed, and then go home. Not if you cared. You wouldn't go home unless you knew the story was right. That meant long hours, and little sleep. It meant that unless you could figure out a way to handle the stress, you would burn out before you were 30. Ben and Janine were both in their 20s, and chances were at least one of them, if not both of them, wouldn't stay in the business much longer. Maybe I could go into public relations, she thought. The money was twice as good, but you had to sell your soul to get the job done, if you worked for a lousy company. Oh well, she thought. Some people do it. Maybe I could too.

Her computer was on and ready to go. Janine let out a long sigh and got back to the present day. She wanted to email Ben a copy of the Queens homicide autopsy report. Her instinct told her he was writing about the same group of people. She opened the file that contained the report, and started scanning it. She hoped she would find anything of interest. She did. The victim had bite marks not only on her neck, but both of her wrists as well. That reflected what Ben had just told her, but it wasn't enough to directly tie the two incidents. Still, she decided to send the report to Ben.

"Just sent it to you Ben!" She yelled across the newsroom.

A minute later, Janine heard a ding from her computer. It was from Rodriguez; a note of thanks.

Janine could follow up. She could walk over to his desk and ask more questions. She could compare notes with him about the two attacks. But she was too tired. She just wanted to go home. Soak in a hot bath; have a glass of wine. Ice cream would be nice, too. In her heart, she knew her hunch was true; the attacks were linked. She shuddered to think about what might have done it. Vampires.

14

Azul had exposed them. He had failed them. To go on a joyride for sport, he had exposed their location to the police and the public. Azul left the museum to hunt for blood, and ended up sucking from a NYPD officer. It was a disaster; the police were almost always to be left untouched. Whenever an officer died, the mayor and the press gave it a lot of coverage. It left questions to be answered, and Man didn't want to take those kinds of risks. You would only drink from one as a last resort, and even then, under special circumstances. Another vampire law had been broken. Azul's recklessness left them totally exposed and in need of another place to bunker.

He was tired of Azul, and this behavior. He just couldn't be trusted anymore. Constantly disobeying orders and putting them in danger. Now, it was time to end him; to retire him. Permanently.

Azul lay on the floor of the museum. He was chained to a desk. Jairoz was standing over him; twisting the chains. Azul grunted and moaned in anguish. "Stop, please!" he screamed out. Man raised his hand, motioning for it to be done again. Jairoz obeyed and twisted the chains once more.

"Why don't you listen to me?" Man asked.

"My lord, please stop! I was hungry. I wanted to get food for all of us! I was looking out for us all!"

Jairoz twisted the chains again, causing Azul to slowly bleed. His blood was purple, like the color of a dark grape. It oozed out of him and onto the floor. Jairoz quickly licked the blood from the floor, to keep it from spreading.

"You have disappointed me Azul. You have disappointed both of us. You have put us all at grave risk, for what purpose? To feed. To satisfy your own lusts. There is nothing more selfish than that."

Man raised his hand. His fingers were like claws, sharp razors that could cut through anything with ease. He slashed at Azul's belly with them, as a tiger fighting in a cage. Azul's stomach emptied onto the floor in front of him. It looked like a pile of pig intestines. The remains of the police officer flopped out onto the floor as Azul wailed in absolute agony.

"SHUT UP!" Man shouted. He leaped onto Azul and slashed at his face, ripping apart eye sockets, hair and dead skin. Azul begged and pleaded for it all to stop, but it was all in vain.

After several minutes, Man slowly raised himself off of Azul. "Jairoz, finish the remains of this man," he said. Jairoz picked up the carcass of the dead police officer and began to feed from it. Scattered around the floor were bits and pieces of what once had been Azul's stomach; along with his eyes and hair.

"Azul, you have lost the trust of your family. You betrayed us by ignoring my orders. As your lord, under our law, I have the right to punish you. Therefore, I condemn you to the curse of the stricken.

You will lie on this floor chained until you starve to death, and then we will consume you."

Azul was too weak to respond. All he could manage was a small whimper. The curse of the stricken was one of the worst punishments that could be administered to a vampire. It was usually reserved for a vampire that had committed mutiny against his or her clan or leader. Azul's transgressions were strong, but hardly seemed equal to mutiny. Still, Man had had enough of him. Azul would die a slow and painful death, being deprived of blood for the rest of his existence. When Man was satisfied that the punishment had run its proper course, Azul's head would be removed.

"My lord, are you sure this is the proper course to take?" Jairoz asked.

"I have loved Azul. The Old One turned him; I trained him. But he has failed us. He has brought danger to our clan. And he will continue to do it if we allow him. I cannot tolerate it any longer."

Jairoz bowed. Man stood over Azul, watching him slowly curl up on the floor. "Leave us Jairoz," Man said. Jairoz walked out.

Azul wouldn't last but a few more hours. It wouldn't be quick, but it would be a relatively painless death now. Azul was so broken he wouldn't feel much of anything more. It was the last gift Man would give to Azul. He had taught him so much, and loved him.

Now, he would stand there and be with him, as long as it would take. Azul would not die alone.

15

The alarm went off at 5 am. Janine tossed around a few times but eventually rustled out of bed. She didn't want to get up this early today, but she had a hunch she needed to. She threw on her old blue jeans and a red hoodie she got from her college bookstore years ago. She shuffled to her front door and opened it, and ran down the three flights of steps to the building's front door. Outside, she walked to the food cart that set up shop on her street corner each morning. For two bucks she could get a cup of coffee and a glazed donut. Breakfast. Then, she walked to the other side of the street, and she found what she was looking for. The Daily Reporter newspaper vending machine was sitting there. She was chomping at the bit to read Rodriguez's story.

Janine got a copy and returned home. She sipped her coffee during the walk upstairs. Inside her apartment, she sat down on the kitchen chair and started to read. It was solid work. Rodriguez definitely picked up on the important elements of the story. The bite marks were on the victims' necks and wrists, which was consistent with all the other incidents. A witness had seen the attack, but the source's name wasn't revealed. Ben had quotes from the MTA and the NYPD, both giving the usual comment about working hard to solve the case.

Janine knew, in her heart, that this must have been the work of Painter's "vampires." They were behind these attacks, just like they had been the culprit in the Queens case she was working on. This was going to happen again; she could feel it. And if the vampires, or whatever they were, were also reading this story, they would know that Rodriguez was a threat. He knew of a witness that had seen them do their work, and they didn't seem to like having witnesses lying around.

She thought too about Painter, and everything he had been telling her over the last several days. He was absolutely convinced of this vampire theory, no matter how hard she tried to dissuade him. Over a bowl of cereal, she compared notes of her interviews with Painter to the story Rodriguez wrote. The witness in the story described seeing more than one attacker. The bite marks were in the same places, but there didn't seem to be any other similarities. Then she found it. The attackers were described as wearing black and having a purple hue on their skin. This fit Painter's description. But none of them were described as being very tall. Could it be a different group of vampires? Jesus, Janine thought, she couldn't believe she was actually starting to believe Painter's crazy rants and ideas. She had never considered herself a believer in conspiracy theories, but there definitely seemed to be some smoke here. Something was going on, and it required more digging. Janine thought maybe she and Rodriguez could start working together on the bite series. Two heads were sometimes better than one.

Janine's cell phone started ringing. Wow, she thought, an early time to be getting a phone call. Must be from work. It was. Joe Zarga was on the other end. Oh

Jesus, she thought, I don't want to have to hear him screaming this early about my stories. She would meet his morning deadline.

"Yes Joe, what's up?"

"Janine, sorry to bother you so early, but I thought you should know. There's been another attack."

"What?"

"An NYPD officer was bludgeoned to death, near the Metropolitan Museum uptown. His body was found in Fort Tryon Park. Bite marks on his neck and wrists."

"Oh shit! That's terrible. Who are you assigning to the story? Rodriguez, or me?"

"There's more bad news. I got a call a little bit ago from Rodriguez's wife. He didn't come home last night."

Janine's body suddenly felt numb. She thought the worst. "Oh God, have you tried calling him?"

"Yes, I'm getting no answer. I know you talked to him last night. Did you get any sense from him that anything was wrong, or that he was going somewhere? I am hoping that maybe he was just chasing a lead down and lost track of time. Or that he's badly hungover after spending all night in some bar. Hell, maybe he fell asleep in some other woman's bed."

Janine spoke more forcefully. "No, Joe, I didn't get a sense that anything was wrong. I sent him a copy of the autopsy report in the Queens case. He didn't say anything to me about any leads. Maybe he went to the city morgue to dig up some new information for his story? I have no idea. I'll try calling him."

"OK. Listen, Gomes, I know you're working this story hard, and I really appreciate it. But be careful, will you? I'm getting concerned that people are realizing our reporters might know a little too much about what's going on."

"Joe. I can take care of myself, but thank you."

There was a pause at the other end of the line.

"Joe, are you there?"

"Yeah. Yeah I'm here. OK. I'm going to go down to the office now, to look around his desk for clues. I'll call his wife too and tell her if he doesn't turn up in the next few hours to phone the police. She hasn't yet. Jesus Christ, what a mess."

"OK. I'll call her as well, to see how she's doing. I'll have those two stories for you around 10 today."

"Thanks Janine. Do you want to cover this latest attack? The cop? I can assign it to somebody else. Howard Grossman is begging for more bylines; he wants to get a job at the Times, I think. I've got him on virus coverage right now."

"Thanks Joe. I'll take it. I'm guessing already from what you've told me it's connected to these other cases. Can I have Beverly with me full-time to help out?"

"That's fine. Take it then. Let's have a web story up on the site as soon as possible. See you soon."

Janine set down her phone and stared at the paper. She couldn't believe it. This situation was totally out of control. The NYPD was constantly playing catch up ball and seemed totally lost in the woods, and now one of their own was targeted. The attacks were happening more consistently than they were the last time, when Painter was on the job. Maybe there are more of them, these vampires he's talking about.

She called Rodriguez's cell. It went straight to voicemail. What was he doing when she left the office last night? He was just writing. That was around 7. He probably finished his story in the next hour, got the edit from Zarga, and sent it to press around 9. That was just a guess, but it was probably in the ballpark. So he's been unaccounted for for nearly 8 hours. It could very well be that he just got drunk and passed out somewhere. She knew that Ben liked to go out for beers with Zarga from time to time. Once she caught them drinking whiskey together in the break room at the newspaper office.

Janine clenched the paper in her hands, till the pages crinkled and ink started to attach itself to her fingers. She'd simply had enough of all of these questions; all of these incidents. It was time to get ahead, instead of staying three or four steps behind. She looked at Painter's interview notes one last time. An abandoned subway tunnel, he said. At 91st street station.

She didn't know what one could find there. But she was going to find out.

16

The newsroom was already buzzing when Janine made it into the office. It was busier than it normally was at 7 am. She had spent the last hour calling Rodriguez but he hadn't answered. She left only one voicemail for him. She hoped everything was alright, but was starting to get a really bad feeling in her gut.

To her surprise, Beverly was waiting for her at her desk as soon as she arrived. Good, Janine thought. We have a lot to do, and she really needed to get some help right away.

"Hey Bev. Thanks for coming in so early."

"I want to help! Is it true that Ben is missing?"

"SHH! Not so loud. I don't know what's going on, but I have heard that yes. Ok, Bev we really have to work this story out." Janine needed to keep Beverly focused. "I need you to write up a summary narrative on what happened for me. Get some drafts of posts too for social media. A narrative on what's happened and what's going to happen with this NYPD officer killing. What do we know?"

"The mayor called a press conference for 9 am. He's going to take some Q and A after he gives a statement. We also got a statement from the governor and the public advocate on the death. The victim was a 20 year veteran of the force. Born, raised in Queens. Left a widow and a young girl."

Janine grimaced. "Oh man, that's awful. Okay, let's post to social media about the press conference right away. I will call the NYPD; try to find out more. I've got to finish banging out another story before 10. An update on the girl killed in Queens."

"Do you think her death and the officer's murder are connected in some way?"

"I don't know for sure, but it wouldn't surprise me."

The televisions in the newsroom turned on. Zarga had arrived. The local news channels were leading with the virus. The governor was increasing restrictions; another cluster of cases were popping up in Westchester, north of the city. A small group of reporters, editors and interns were starting to crowd around and watch the coverage. So much for social distancing. At least everyone was wearing a mask. The voices got louder, as Beverly started asking Janine more questions. She couldn't hear over the sounds of the TVs.

"What was that Bev? Sorry I can't hear you."

"I said are you going to the press conference? We've got to get on the press attendance list if you're going."

Janine looked at the newsroom clock. Just after 7. 10 am news deadline on two stories, and the press conference at 9. There was just too much going on already. She frowned.

"No, I can't. I have to finish these two stories for Zarga, and he hasn't changed the deadline on me. I have to finish writing. Start the stream for me, will you? Record it too, and take some notes for me on important places to look for quotes and background. In the meantime, post to social media about the 9 o'clock presser. And whatever statements we're getting from officials."

"Sure Janine." Bev was writing down her list of assignments in a reporter's notebook.

"Thanks Bev. You're fantastic. Also, see where the cop was from in Queens. Maybe we can ask around his old neighborhood, get somebody who knew him or worked with him for a feature."

Bev wrote it down and started to head over to the intern desk. Janine pulled out her phone to call Rodriguez again.

"You've reached the cell phone of Ben Rodriguez..."

Janine put her phone away. She sat down at her desk and started writing. She sensed she was being watched again. She lifted her head and Doug Cross was standing there. Janine nearly jumped out of her chair.

"Sorry Janine. Didn't mean to frighten you. We're having a newsroom meeting in the conference room in ten minutes. Full time employees only."

"Thanks Doug. How are you doing?"

"OK. Things are really tough. My mother in law lives up in Westchester, near where this outbreak is happening. She's basically just staying in her house. My wife wants to go up there this weekend, but apparently the governor is going to set up some sort of sealed off area or something."

Janine shuddered at the thought of it. Society seemed to be falling apart. She started rubbing her temples as Doug started talking about his wife and kids. He was going through a divorce, and it was a painful one. Janine didn't really care to hear any of it.

"Thanks Doug for letting me know. Hope your mother in law's okay. I will see you in there."

Doug walked away as Janine started writing again. She couldn't get Painter's words out of her mind. Every minute she was sitting in the newsroom, another killing could be happening. She had to get out of there and try her luck at 91st street. But if she went in there without protecting herself, she could be killed. She was certain someone was down there, but definitely not a vampire. Still, Painter sounded very convincing. Her mind drifted toward the subway, and whatever may be lurking there. Her newsroom phone was ringing, and she couldn't hear it. It took three rings for her to snap back to reality. She answered. It was Joe Zarga.

"Janine, newsroom meeting in the conference room. Be there in about ten. How are the stories coming?"

"Fine. I've got Beverly covering the NYPD officer's death for social media. She's recording the mayor's press conference this morning for me. I'll have a web story on that later this afternoon, too. I'll be done with these other stories for tomorrow's paper this morning. I'll have it done ahead of 10 am."

"OK. See you in a few."

***

The paper's conference room was used once a week for big news meetings, but didn't get much use outside of that. Once in a while, a big name from out of town would stop by and use it to meet with Zarga and other editors. They always wanted to see the offices because they were thinking of buying the paper. To make a few bucks, the newsroom would sometimes do tours on weekends too so the public could see the offices. The sports department would have meetings there sometimes before big games, to coordinate coverage. Zarga liked to walk around the newsroom to get story pitches and ideas, and give out direction. He hated the ambience of the cold and dreary conference room, with its dilapidating chairs and outdated technical equipment. That's what made this news meeting all the more interesting to Janine.

Janine sat in a corner, far away from Zarga. She clasped onto her reporter's notebook and brought a yellow legal pad as well for notes. Howard Grossman sat next to Zarga. Clearly a strategic move; he wanted to be a teacher's pet. Doug sat across from her. Janine could see the sports reporters; arts and cultural team; cops and courts folks. All of the editors were there as well. Sadly, she noticed Ben Rodriugez wasn't there. Her heart sank.

"Guys, we have to spread out. You're sitting too close, Howard. Sorry to call you out, but we have to spread out. See if you can get six feet between you. Social distance, guys," Zarga said. Zarga looked around, directing traffic. He ordered one of the younger reporters to open the conference room door. "If you can't fit in here, gather just outside the door ladies and gentlemen. I'm sorry but we have to be safe. And put your masks on, please!"

Janine noticed a few of the sports people didn't have masks. They ran back to their desks to get them. Zarga impatiently waited for them to return before speaking again.

"OK guys, I have an announcement to make," Zarga started. "First, I have some very bad news. I'm sad to say that Ben Rodriguez is missing."

This caused a very loud stir in the room. There were gasps and murmurs, and Doug Cross gave Janine a worried glance. Janine felt very uncomfortable.

"How long has he been missing? I saw him yesterday!" Doug said.

"I don't want to go into much detail, because I just don't have a lot of details. He was here last night," Zarga replied. "But I got a call from his wife this morning. He hadn't come home. He left here around 9:30 last night. His wife's not been able to reach him, so she's contacting the police."

More stirring. Doug Cross looked very uncomfortable. One of the other editors, Teresa Ice, started to cry.

"Please guys, let's not have a panic. We don't know that anything is wrong. It's just that he hasn't been in contact with anyone. Please, if Ben contacts any of you, let me know. His wife is very worried, and so am I. So let's please remain calm, and do our jobs."

There was a tense silence in the room. Zarga quickly switched subjects to try and salvage the meeting and the group's morale. "OK, now in regards to coverage-- it looks like this virus is taking a heavy toll on the city. We know we have cases here, and there's also the mess up in Westchester. Teresa, you're editor of metro. I want you guys in metro to cover the Westchester stories, from every angle we can. Let's send someone up there."

"OK Joe, who do you want?" Teresa asked.

"I'll do it Joe," Grossman said. What a kiss ass, Janine thought. This asshole has been floating from paper to paper for years. He couldn't hold down a job. Janine scowled at him.

"Fine," Zarga said. "Howard, head up there today. They're apparently setting up a drive through testing site with the help of the National Guard. Let's start working those sources. Also, call the town's mayor. What's the name of the town that's getting hit?"

"New Rochelle," Doug said.

"OK. Howard, call the mayor of New Rochelle. We want to talk to them, but also business owners, city council members, even the dogcatcher if we can. Run your stories through with Teresa, I want something in print tomorrow."

"Got it," Grossman replied.

"Now, in regards to city coverage, with the virus. Teresa, I want a reporter and an intern working this as well. I'm open to suggestions."

"OK. Erica's been covering it up to now. I suggest we stay with her," Teresa said. She pointed over to Erica Hartman, a 25 year old brunette girl from Paducah, Kentucky. Erica was the newest reporter added to the staff. She was only about six months out of Northwestern journalism school. Janine didn't think she was ready to handle it, but in light of the tension in the room already, she chose not to add to it.

"Erica, think you can handle it? It's okay if you say no," Zarga replied. Janine could tell Joe was hoping she would take a pass on it.

"I'm ready for it Mr. Zarga," Erica replied.

"OK. How about Beverly working with you too as your intern," Zarga said.

"No Joe," Janine chimed in finally. "Bev's working with me on the bite attacks series."

Zarga frowned. "Oh yes," he said. "We may need to switch you over, Janine, to help Erica with virus coverage. This story is building up more and more. I am hearing they may even have Broadway theater houses shut down. That hasn't happened in I don't know how long. Maybe it's never happened. This story is starting to spill over into every aspect of life. Sports, I want you guys to cover how it's affecting March Madness-"

"Joe, wait," Janine interrupted. "The bite attacks are just as important. We have a crime wave happening throughout Manhattan, and we're the ONE paper as far as I can tell that's putting a lot of time and effort into it."

"Janine we just don't have the resources-"

"Yes, we do Joe. Keep me and Bev on this story. I have probably the most structure and background on this than any other reporter in the city."

"We're already down one reporter-"

"Joe, we have no idea what happened to Ben, for all we know he'll walk into this meeting in five minutes. I'm telling you, I have a source that's helping me get-"

"Janine."

"Fantastic background research, I'm going to explore a really important lead today--"

"Miss Gomes."

"And by the end of the day we may be able to get everything we need on this-"

"MISS GOMES!"

Zarga roared like a lion in the jungle. It shut down the entire room. You could hear a needle drop, as Janine burned with anger and frustration. Her face got cherry red. She was about to push Zarga even more, but he wouldn't let her back in the conversation.

"Janine, I know you've got two stories you're wrapping up today and I do need you to finish those. I also need you to give some coverage to the NYPD officer who was killed. As of today, you're still on the attacks. Beverly will help you. We're just going to have to keep our eyes and ears open with this virus story and how to handle it. Erica, you're leading on that. Take one of the other interns to help you. Whoever Teresa approves. When Ben comes back, hopefully that's today, he can work on that as well."

Janine zoned out as Zarga continued to drone on to the newsroom about what he wanted from them. She tried her best to breathe deeply and get over her anger at Zarga. She couldn't believe he was actually thinking of pulling her off the biggest crime story the city's seen in decades. She closed her eyes and imagined a sandy beach, to help her center herself. After more deep breathing, she was able to get back into the moment. She knew in her heart that Zarga probably didn't want her off the story, but his options were limited since Ben was missing. Oh God, she thought. Ben, please get back here. Please be okay. We need you.

"Okay, one last thing," Zarga continued. "The governor's expected to announce new restrictions on how many employees can work from the office, and how many must work from home. We're expecting an announcement today that half of a company's workforce must be working from home, starting tomorrow."

More gasps and loud murmurs filled the room. Zarga raised his hand as he started speaking again.

"But," Zarga said, "the governor's chief of staff told me that news organizations are exempt. However, we are going to have all of our editors, starting tomorrow, working from home. You'll be corresponding with reporters and me through email and phone. I will be working from the office to help with operations of the paper. The only people reporting to work will be reporters who are working on virus coverage. That's Erica, Ben, Janine, Howard, and myself. Also, we will have fewer people working on press. Advertising staff is going to be working from home. And we're sadly going to have fewer delivery drivers. At this time, our interns also will be working from home. Also, everyone who is reporting to work must wear a mask AT ALL TIMES, and they must also wear plastic gloves for the time being at all times."

Janine listened as Zarga went on, but she started putting together a game plan in her head. Beverly wouldn't be around to help her, but she could still use her to make phone calls and arrange interviews if necessary. That was good. She also wouldn't have to answer too many questions about where she was going or where she had just come from. That was certainly a good thing. She just had to get out of the meeting, so she could get all the wheels in motion.

It took another thirty minutes for the tedious meeting to end. Finally, Zarga dismissed the room and Janine rushed to get to the door, so she wouldn't have to get a lecture from her boss on newsroom etiquette. She raced to her desk and Beverly was there, with a notepad in hand.

"Bev, I don't have time. I'm sorry I have to finish these stories, can someone else help you?"

"Janine, Ben's wife keeps calling. He hasn't come home. She is in a panic."

"Okay, if she calls again put her through directly to Zarga. That's not your job to deal with her."

"OK. I have some posts ready to go up on social media. Do you want to look at them before I put them through?"

"I'm sorry, I just can't right now. Have Zarga look at them. It's his final call, anyway."

Beverly walked away and Janine sat down at her desk. As soon as she started typing on her computer the desk phone rang. The caller ID said Joe Zarga. He undoubtedly wanted to chew her out for clashing with him at the meeting. Here we go, she thought. She answered the phone.

"GET IN MY OFFICE. NOW," Zarga whispered intensely through the telephone.

"I'm writing Joe. I'll be done with this story-"

"THIS ISN'T A NEGOTIATION!"

His voice sounded shrill and she could tell he was barely able to keep his composure. She just decided to quit fighting.

"Got it. Be right there." She hung up right away to keep him from saying anything else.

Janine stood and shuffled some of her papers on her desk. She was trying to delay, but also to keep her mind centered. She had to be prepared for this showdown. She grabbed her reporter's notebook and a blue pen, to take notes.

The lights were on in Zarga's office, but the door was closed and the blinds were drawn. She knocked and went right in. Zarga sat behind his desk, wearing his glasses and the morning's paper was strewn all around him. There was a coffee ring on the sports page, where he had placed his cup. Joe loved baseball. He was a huge Yankees fan, but he didn't read much else in the sports section usually except for the box scores. Once she saw him enter the newsroom and throw the sports section of the paper right in the wastebasket. She was surprised that a news man would ignore such a huge section of the news business.

"SIT DOWN." Zarga was definitely still pissed at her. He removed his glasses and rubbed his eyes.

Janine did as she was told. She wanted to just jump right in and defend herself, but she decided against it. This argument was going to be like a chess match, and Zarga essentially had her in check because he was her boss. With a snap of his fingers, he could take her off the most important story she had covered in her young career, and put her on virus coverage. That was important too, but she knew that no one else in the city had access to the information she held in her possession. If she played her cards right, she could get a huge promotion and bring a lot of good publicity to the paper. Maybe she'd even get an award, like a Pulitzer Prize. That was the most respected honor in the world of print journalism.

"Janine, I don't really give a shit about what your feelings are on this story," Zarga said. He put his glasses back on. "But let me tell you something. I'm the executive editor here, and you work for me. You're talented. You're smart. You've got a long career ahead of you in the news business. But you need to learn to go along, and get along. There are at least three other people on my staff with more experience than you. Grossman being one of them, and he's getting the shittiest assignment, of all of you."

"OK."

"No, Janine, just listen. I trust your news sense, I do. Your stories are solid, for the most part. I think that you're right with this bite series. It is important. But this virus is going to rip apart society as we know it. I have been talking to some doctors and my contact at the CDC. We don't know what's about to hit us. This is an all hands on deck situation, and I need the crew to get in line and get the job done here. And now we've got Ben missing, and his wife scared out of her wits. She's calling me, looking to me for help. What can I do? I have no idea what's happened to Ben. She's filing a missing person's report with the police."

Zarga was worried. Janine could tell, because he started playing with his glasses again. Janine took a moment to think about what he'd said.

"Oh Jesus. That's terrible news."

"Yes. It is. So Janine, please, just do me a favor and get in line to help ok? You can have today to finish your series, but tomorrow, I need you working on virus coverage. I need you to contact the labor department and do a story on how they are going to be handling the unemployment claims."

"Really? How do you mean?"

"It looks like the city is headed toward a lockdown. No Broadway shows, no offices open, and no restaurants open either. Sporting games canceled. A total shut down."

"Holy shit, Joe, that's crazy. The CDC thinks that's what's going to happen?"

"Confidentially, yes. China got slammed by this thing, and there's no vaccine. We know that it's in the city. First, there was that nurse who had it. And then Westchester becomes a hotspot. It's just a matter of time before the cases spike in the city. No one is going to want to ride the subway anymore."

"Wow."

"Exactly. So finish this bite series today. Take all the time you need today, but get it done. Let's knock out the Queens killing update, this morning. Then the NYPD officer, let's get that piece online by early this afternoon. Then take the rest of the day to work on whatever else you wanted to write about with the bite series. Have Beverly assigned to whatever you need. I'll put your stuff on the front page tomorrow, below the fold."

"Who is top priority?"

"Maybe Grossman, maybe it's Erica. Either way the virus is going above the fold tomorrow. And the day after, too. Who knows how long after that."

"It's still an important story, Joe. These bite attacks are going to keep happening."

"I know. I hope you're wrong. But if we are both right, the story will still be there for you to pick up again when we don't need you for virus coverage."

"But what about Ben? If he shows up today, you can throw that unemployment piece to him."

"I don't know Janine. I am starting to freak out a little about him. Something's wrong. His wife hasn't heard from him. It's been nearly 12 hours, and Ben wouldn't go that long without speaking to his wife. They have a child together."

"I know Joe. I know. That's just....really screwed up. He didn't say anything to you about where he was going after he left the office?"

Zarga shook his head. "No," he said. "Didn't say a word, other than how much he missed his kid. That's why I know something's wrong. He loved that baby."

Janine looked at the floor. She could see Ben's face in her mind, and the face of his wife. She didn't know them well, but they seemed like honest people.

"Joe, I need to go out for a few hours, there's a source I need to speak to about the series."

"This is your anonymous source?"

"Yes, in a way. It's complicated. But it's someone very important. I need some time to shake them down, and figure a few things out. You'll have your stuff before the end of the day. I'll make the deadline."

Janine stood up and walked out of Zarga's office. She had to get to 91st-and find out for certain if what Painter had been saying was true.

17

Ben Rodriguez lie crumpled on the museum floor. His head had a lump on it the size of a grapefruit, from where they had beaten him. He was bleeding from his head, but also from his wrists. He couldn't remember how he had gotten there. He was walking home from the subway, he did remember that. He had had a few drinks at the bar near his place, and was about to get to his front door. Then something happened. That was all he could remember.

The museum was cold and damp. He shivered while lying on the floor. His coat had been taken from him, and he wasn't wearing many layers. His sweater had been soaked in his blood, and his chinos had been soiled. He was very hungry and needed to relieve himself. He yelled, and screamed for help, but no one came. Someone must have put him here, but he didn't know who.

It was dark where he was. He couldn't see very far in front of him. Only a few feet. He could just make out his shoes in the black abyss. Finally, after what seemed like hours of shouting, a door opened. It was from far down a hall. Two figures, dark in color, wearing what looked like black trench coats, walked towards him. He shuddered while looking at them. One was medium in height and seemed overweight. The other was tall and lean, with a scar on his right cheek. They glared at him as they approached.

"Benjamin Rodriguez, I hope you are feeling better," the Man said. "You gave us quite a fight when we took you. I'm sorry about the bump on your head."

"Who are you?" Rodriguez asked.

"I am what you want me to be; a friend, or an enemy. If you answer my questions and cooperate with me, I will be your friend. And if you don't, then you will force me to become your enemy."

"What are you talking about? What do you want?"

"You wrote a story in the newspaper, the Daily Reporter. In it, you wrote that a witness described the attacks on the subway to you. I want you to tell me, who was this witness?"

"Why?"

"The more you procrastinate, the worse you will feel Benjamin. Why don't you just answer the question."

"I don't see it as any of your business. Besides, I would never reveal a source's name to anyone. What are you? Mafia?"

Man smiled at him. "No Benjamin. I'm something much worse." He nodded at Jairoz. Jairoz struck Rodriguez across the face. Ben's face swung sideways like a screen door, and two of his teeth flew across the room. He whimpered in pain and fell to the floor.

Man stood over him. "Don't try and play the martyr. Just tell me what I want to know, Benjamin. I will spare you."

"Spare me from what?"

"From pain. From feeling the most incredible amounts of pain."

Man placed his hand on Rodriguez's shoulder. A sharp, intense pain started to drip itself inside of him. It consumed him. It moved through him, and he surrendered to it. He groaned in agony as it touched each nerve, each muscle, each bone. Man smiled.

"This is just a taste, Benjamin. I can make this much worse for you. Now, tell me."

He removed his hand from Ben' shoulder. Ben gasped for air as he wriggled slowly on the ground. He tried to move away, but Man wouldn't let him escape.

"You're pathetic, look at you. Crawling along the ground like a dog. Just disgusting," Man said. He kicked Ben hard in the ribs, and Ben released a bloodcurdling scream that seemed to shake the entire building. "Watch the door," Man said. Jairoz left the room. Man took a few steps away from Ben, watching him carefully with his piercing grey eyes.

"I know a lot about you Mr. Rodriguez," Man said. I know about your wife; your young child. A beautiful baby."

"Fuck you," Ben whispered.

Man laughed. "I admire your courage, I do. Mr. Rodriguez, you certainly have a great deal of it," he said. "But why kill yourself over this? Just tell me the name. Tell me who the witness is. And you will be released. You have my word."

Ben tried to speak, but his pain was too great. He slowly moved into a fetal position. He held his ribs. There was a break. He breathed slowly, then deeply. Slowly, then deeply again.

"Why should I trust you?" Ben whispered.

"Because you have seen what I can do," Man said. "And you've just tasted the tip of the iceberg, Mr. Rodriguez. I swear to you. There are fates worse than death, and I can show you that, if you don't cooperate with me."

"I don' t believe you."

"Very well, I will show you." Man got down on his hands and knees. He dipped his head into the small pool of Ben's blood that had gathered on the floor. Man started licking it and then slowly began slurping it up, like a dog. Rodriguez could feel pain returning inside of him. His body jerked around on the floor, writhing in agony unlike anything he had ever felt before. He tried to scream but was too weak to make any sounds. His body seemed to be shutting down, and this thing wasn't even touching him. He couldn't understand it.

Man lifted his head. His mouth was covered in Rodriguez's blood. He smiled at him. "Now do you believe?" he asked. Ben's eyes widened in horror. Man stood up and towered over him. Rodriguez lay there terrified. He stared into the eyes of the ghoul; paralyzed in fear.

"I can do anything I want to you Mr. Rodriguez. I can kill you, but I don't want to. At least not yet. I can drink your blood, but there's something much worse I can do to you. I can force you to drink blood like me. To become like me; to serve me. You would never see your family again. Is that what you want?"

Rodriguez whimpered. He wet himself on the floor. A pool of urine began to form all around his limp body.

Man smiled again. "Don't play the role of a hero. You've proven your bravery to me; you have my respect. For a human, you are quite magnificent. I will give you six hours, Mr. Rodriguez, to decide. At dusk, you will be forced to make a decision. Reveal the name of your source to me, or face a fate that is worse than death. Eternal separation from the ones you love."

Rodriguez started tearing up.

"I will bring you some food. And water. If you have to relieve yourself, I'm afraid that you will have to just do that right here," Man said. "Think carefully, Mr. Rodriguez."

Man stood and slowly turned away from him. Ben passed out from his pain before Man had even reached the door at the end of the hallway.

18

Janine stood at the corner of the platform at 96th street and Broadway. The stench of the subway tunnel filled her nostrils. It smelled of dirt, grime, sweat and dust. In two minutes, a train would arrive heading uptown. As soon as that one was gone, she had seven minutes to run down the tunnel before the next one arrived. Janine stood next to the ladder leading down to the tracks, looking all around her. There were a few people on the platform, but no one was close to her. Social distancing would actually be to her advantage.

Janine put on her mask. She had her reporter's notebook, as well as a knife and pepper spray she brought to protect herself. She could see the lights of the train coming toward her. It was about to arrive in the station. She had gone over this scenario in her head all morning. This was her last chance to turn back, to remain standing in front of the looking glass. She thought about Painter, and everything he had said to her. She still didn't believe in vampires, but she knew it was a lead that needed to be explored. They were probably just junkies who thought they were vampires. She had read once in the Times about an underground sex community in New York that liked to bite and suck on each other, pretending they were vampires. This was probably something like that.

The train whooshed by her as it pulled into the station. It was nearly empty. The virus was keeping people away, and today that was going to work to her advantage. It was illegal to go down on the tracks. She had to try and stay as covert as possible.

The doors on the train opened. A homeless man was sitting down in the subway car, with a shopping cart full of possessions. It contained mostly empty soda pop cans. Their eyes met. He smiled and lifted his arm, pointing at her. Janine gave him a puzzled glance. He started laughing. Janine realized he was laughing at her mask. The doors closed. Janine gave him the finger and waved at the man. He stopped laughing and gave her the finger back. Janine smirked as the train pulled out of the station.

"Alright, let's do this," she said.

Janine climbed down the ladder and leapt onto the tracks. She could still smell the brakes from the train that had passed. She glanced around. There were markings on the tunnel walls from where the MTA workers had taken readings and did measurements for equipment. She couldn't make out anything else. She could tell that she was surrounded by dirt, grime and dust. It was disgusting. She clenched her fists. She had to quickly regain her focus. She looked in front of her, into the tunnel going downtown, but couldn't see anything. Good. The next train wasn't in sight yet. She pulled out her cell phone and turned on the flashlight. She started running down the tunnel, as hard as she could.

Blue neon lights were scattered along the track, and it helped Janine to find her footing in the tunnel. She stopped for a moment to catch her breath. She checked behind her. No one was there. She glanced around for rats. There were none around. She could barely make out the platform at 96th street. She

102

couldn't tell if anyone noticed her fall down to the tracks. She had to keep going, she kept telling herself. Just keep moving forward.

Janine turned to stare again down the tunnel into the darkness. She wasn't far from the abandoned station. She tried to remember everything Painter had told her about it. There wasn't much to remember. She cursed herself for not asking him more about what she could find, what she should expect to see. She started running again down the tunnel. She could see white graffiti sprayed on the walls; some type of symbols. Faster, run faster, she thought. She still couldn't see the train that was supposed to be arriving next. That made her feel a little better.

She moved past more graffiti, and suddenly she saw a yellow strip on the wall. It was some type of opening, on her left. It was also well lit. She slowed down just before the crevice, and tried to creep up to it, but she had been running too fast. A cramp was developing in her knee from running so hard. Damn, she thought, I need to work out more.

Janine turned to look down the opening. It was a service tunnel. A brown door looked welded shut right next to the service tunnel entrance. There was puke green graffiti paint sprayed over the walls, along with off white and red. Electric boxes aligned the wall on the left side. She could see stairs in the distance, leading up to the street. Janine gulped. This must have been where Painter followed the figure into the tunnel, all those years ago. This must be the place where Painter's source had led him. The floors of the side tunnel weren't as grimy or dusty as the track. In fact, it was lit pretty well considering this was next to an abandoned station. Janine decided to stop and catch her breath. As she stood there, she started cursing herself again. Why did she come alone? She should have brought someone with her to help, in case there was more than one person down here lurking. She had taken protective measures, but would they be enough if she needed it? She closed her eyes. Suddenly, she heard a rumbling coming from outside on the tracks. It must have been the next train arriving at 86th street. Janine looked to her left out onto the tracks. Should she chance it and run to 91st? She might be seen by the train conductor. Or worse, she might be hit by the train. There wasn't much room between the wall of the tunnel and the actual tracks. It would be a tight fit.

Janine decided to stay put until the train passed. She took out her reporter's notebook and looked over notes Painter had given her about the people he had met down here. Purple hue to their skin. Dressed in black. The leader was very tall and extremely gaunt. She closed her eyes, and tried to picture him. She kept thinking back to an old vampire movie her mother liked when she was little. Willem Dafoe was in it, she remembered, and he was playing a vampire disguised as an actor. He looked terrifying, she remembered. Janine quickly searched her pockets for the pepper spray. She found it, and clasped onto it. She should be armed before she made her final leg of the journey.

The rumbling got louder. The train had left 86th and was chugging along uptown to get to 96. Louder, and louder. She could hear the brakes; she could smell the train car pressing itself down onto the old subway tracks. Then she saw it on her left. The silver hue of the train, pushing its way past the service tunnel where she was hiding. Fortunately, she couldn't see up into the actual car, where people would be sitting. That meant they couldn't see her, either. She sighed a sigh of relief as the train passed her by and moved ahead to 96th.

As soon as it moved through, Janine looked out toward 91st. She couldn't see anything. She couldn't hear anyone, either. She decided to start running again, as she left the passageway. She passed more graffiti in red and white as she made her way back down the tunnel. Lights hung near the ceiling, lighting her way. The tunnel seemed to go on forever and ever, so she slowed down. She held her side as she walked forward. Then she saw it. The floor of the tunnel stopped and dark brown steps were in front of her. She had made it. This was the abandoned station at 91st.

She stopped right before she reached the station platform. She could hear a train moving in the distance, coming from 96th and going downtown. That would be on the other side of the tracks. She couldn't hear anything else, and she couldn't see either. She reached into her pocket for her phone to get her flashlight. Her hands were slippery from sweating, and as she brought the phone out of her pocket it slipped from her hands and fell down near the tracks. "Shit!" she yelled. She quickly froze. Her cover was blown. If someone or something was there, it surely would have heard her by now.

Janine went down to the tracks carefully to find her phone. There was no point in trying to hide now. The floor was a sea of black, as the station platform engulfed the floor from getting any light. She would have to get on her hands and knees to feel around for her phone. "Oh God," she muttered to herself. Her greatest fear wasn't getting dirty. It was getting gnawed by rats. They ran amok in the subway tunnels. She couldn't wait forever to find the phone, she kept telling herself. Time was ticking against her. She knelt down, examining the darkened area by the platform. Her phone was somewhere in this abyss. Suddenly, a light flashed on the tracks. It was her phone! She had received a text message that had lit up the screen. She quickly ran over to it. Her screen was cracked, but the phone seemed to be alright.

Janine wiped her phone with an old tissue she found in one of her pockets. The text was from Zarga. He wanted to know how things were going on her story about the slain NYPD officer. She just couldn't escape his micromanaging, even in an abandoned subway station.

Janine turned her flashlight back on and waved it around the 91st street platform. It was a small station platform, built to handle smaller trains. That's why it wasn't used anymore. It had been out of commission she read since the 1950s. There was graffiti all over the walls; neon colors, and letters that looked like they were written in cursive. It was actually very pretty. Janine thought it looked like an art exhibit she had seen a long time ago at the Brooklyn museum that showcased 1980s graffiti artists in the city.

Janine shined her light back on the platform. There were large beams near the stairs blocking her view. She couldn't make out anything else. She pulled out her pepper spray and held it in her left hand as she made her way back to the platform stairs. She held her phone with the flashlight guiding the way, with her right hand. She carefully climbed the platform stairs. They were stable. The MTA probably still used this platform for maintenance, she thought.

The platform was desolate. There was a white bag leaning next to one of its walls, but nothing else. Steps in one corner that would have led up to the street when the station was in service. She walked over to the walls, studying the graffiti markings. It didn't look like anyone lived here. She stared at the other side of the tracks, on the platform going downtown.

Then she saw it. Something. A figure was standing on the other side of the tracks, on the downtown platform. She was on the wrong side! "HEY!" She yelled at the figure. A train was coming on the express track, heading uptown, right in the middle of the subway tracks. It would soon block her view of the other side of the platform. "Hey, wait! Just wait right there!" Janine yelled, but it was too late. The express train was too close to the station, and the sound muffled out the sound of her voice. She tried to wave at the figure but the train got in the way, sprinting to 96th street from 72nd. It was too late.

The train passed by so loudly that Janine had to cover her ears. She kept staring as best she could at the spot where she saw the figure. When the train had gone, the figure went with it. It had disappeared from the spot. Janine quickly looked to her left, down the tunnel. A train was about to pass 91st street on the uptown local track. She wanted to make a run for it to try and cross the tracks, but it would be too hard to do that in the darkness. She would have to wait until the train passed. "Son of a bitch," she muttered to herself, slapping her hand against her knee. Janine did that sometimes when she was really frustrated. This was certainly one of those moments.

Janine's phone vibrated. She held it to her face. It was Zarga. "Oh dear God, what is this man's problem?" she said. As she pulled the phone away, the light shone on the figure. It was right in front of her. She screamed. A bystander on a nearby platform may have heard her, but another express train heading the opposite direction muffled out the sound.

***

When Janine awoke she was lying down on the 91st street station steps, the ones leading up to the street. It was as dark as the blackest night she'd ever seen. She couldn't see her hand in front of her face. She tried to get up, but something seemed to be weighing her down. Her legs wouldn't move.

108

"Why are you here?"

Janine froze. The voice was coming from somewhere on the other side of the platform, but she couldn't see anything. It was low and hissed like a snake. It curdled her blood.

"Answerrrr me."

Janine stuttered, trying to form some words. For the first time in as long as she could remember, she was absolutely terrified.

"I...I am looking for someone," she managed to whisper. "I...I...was...sent, I was sent here to find someone."

"Who sssent you here?"

"He's someone who used to write about what happened at this station. Yuh, yuh, years ago. He's someone who knew the mole people."

"Give me the nnnnnnnnname."

Janine tried to fight it, with all of her might. She started tearing up. She didn't want to reveal the name of Painter. It was against her ethics as a journalist. A reporter needed to protect their sources. But then she remembered what Painter had said, that he wanted to atone for the sins he had committed. Janine made her choice, then and there.

"P...Painter. His name is Gregory Painter. Please don't hurt me. I'm not here to harm you. I'm trying to find the...the person who he knew that lived here."

"Where is the strega?"

"Who? What...what are you talking about?"

"The witch. The witch who brought Painter hereeee. Did the witch send you to me?"

"Nnn....No sir. Painter sent me here. I'm here because I'm writing.....I'm writing a story for the Daily Reporter about the attacks, the bite attacks that are happ...happening in the city."

There was silence. It went on, and on, for what seemed like a century. Janine tried to sit up, but her legs wouldn't let her. She moved her hands in the darkness to feel her legs. They seemed fine, but they wouldn't lift. There was no weight on them, but something, something was holding her there.

"What do you wanttt with me?"

"I am trying...trying to find who caused these attacks. They are similar to what happened, yuh, years ago. Painter told me that years ago, when this happened before, that....that vampires were at this place. That he helped them, and protected them."

Silence again. She could feel this figure, this ghoul, thinking about what she had been telling him. She could feel his eyes on her, watching her, trying to determine if she was telling the truth. She could then hear it moving. It was moving closer to her. She couldn't see it, but she knew it was there. She could smell something. It was the breath of the figure. It smelled like what she imagined a rotting corpse would smell like. Or a mountain of sewage and trash that had been dumped at a landfill on Staten Island. Janine gagged. She gagged again. She thought she would vomit.

"Breathee.....deeply. It will help calm youuuu."

Janine closed her eyes. She tried to breathe deeply, but couldn't. She was having a panic attack. She wanted to scream, but nothing came out.

"Breatheeeee......"

Janine took short breaths, in and out. In and out. Then she started gulping in more air, and breathing a bit deeper. This happened again and again. She finally started to calm down. She tried to look at the figure, but it was too dark and he was too far away.

"Sir," she began, "Painter sent me here. He hoped you could help me. He told me that he helped you before,when these types of attacks were taking place decades ago. I...I was hoping you would know what was happening."

"Youuuu are very brave, to come here alone. You are also very reckless. Why should I help youuu?"

"I......don't have an answer for that sir. I'm sorry. But people are dying and I plead to you that if you can do something to stop them, the city would be very grateful."

The figure's voice changed. It sounded richer and clearer.

"I want to be left alone. I always have. Painter brought a lot of trouble for me, and I had hoped I would never have to deal with him again."

"He isn't here. He hasn't told anyone about you.....other than me. He's sick, he wants to make peace with himself for things he's said he's done."

"He is a coward, to send you here alone against me. Didn't he tell you what I am, what I am capable of?"

"He said you were....a vampire."

The figure walked closer to Janine. She could see his outline, just a sketch of it settled in the vast darkness. She could feel his eyes piercing through her again. She could smell the rotten smell of his breath again, mixed in with the sweat, dust and grime of the crumbling subway station. Janine reached down to her pockets, hoping to find the pepper spray. It was gone.

"He told you that...and still you came to see me?"

"Yes."

"Then you are far braver than I give you credit for. What is your name?"

"My name is Janine Gomes. I'm a journalist for the New York Daily Reporter. The same paper that Painter worked for. What's your name? Painter didn't tell me."

"Don't worry about my name. What do you want from me?"

"Do you know who's causing the bite attacks happening in the city?"

"Perhaps."

"What does that mean?"

"I live here, I stay here, Miss Gomes. I don't go out. I don't read newspapers. So I cannot say for certain I know who is doing this."

"But you knew the last time?"

"You tire me."

"I'm sorry, but I really need your help! Please, what can you tell me about what happened before?"

"I am weak Miss. I have lived off of rats and feral cats for a very long time. If I were to help you, I would need to replenish my strength."

"What do you mean?"

"I do not carry the strength to do what you ask. I must taste human flesh. I must have human blood. Once I have drank, then I will be able to help you. But you must help me first."

"You mean drink my blood?" Janine raised her voice.

The figure laughed. "You are certainly human. But I didn't mean you. Still, you must help me drink."

"How?"

"Miss Gomes, if you want my help, you must help me first. You must bring me a human, to drink from."

"WHAT? You're insane!"

The figure laughed again. "This is the way we are made, Miss Gomes. Vampires drink human blood. Not all stories of fiction are actually fiction, you know."

"But why do I have to bring you a human?"

"As I said, I am very weak. I haven't left this platform in many years. Since I lost contact with the strega. I have had no one to help me hunt. You want me to help you, to trust you? Then do this for me. Give me human flesh, and I swear to you I will help you in what you seek."

"I can't do that. You're asking me to help you in killing someone."

"I understand. I respect you Miss Gomes, for having principles. But you will learn, in order to survive, you must compromise on them from time to time. If you change your mind, on the next full moon bring a human at midnight, to the rock in Inwood Hill Park. It's called Shorakkopoch Rock. You know it?"

"No."

"It's a holy place for my kind. It's there that if we drink human blood, we will be blessed with the strength and power of 100 vampires."

"Like a charging station?"

"So to speak. Once a vampire heals there, they cannot do it again for 100 years."

"And you've been waiting for your turn?"

"For a very long time. So Miss Gomes, if you want my help, that is what you must do. Now, leave this place." The figure moved farther and farther away from her, gliding toward the station stairs.

"Wait," she said as she was finally able to get up, "what do you call yourself? What's your name?"

"I am called the Old One."

19

Man stared out of one of the windows at the museum, looking at the flowers that had been planted in front of the entrance. He loved the smell of flowers, when he was human. He couldn't smell them anymore. Now he could only smell the blood that he craved in order to survive. He could smell human flesh; he knew when one was ripe for eating and when one was sick, and shouldn't be eaten. Still, he liked to look at flowers. It helped calm him.

Man couldn't remember much from his time as a human. He did however remember how much he liked flowers, because his mother had a garden. He would sit with her while she pruned rose bushes in their yard. He would laugh a lot with her, while they worked on the roses. It wasn't really their yard; it belonged to another man, a very powerful man, that his mother worked for. It didn't matter to Man, it felt like their own place. Their own house. He'd also help weed the garden bed in the summer season. Summer was his favorite season, before he was turned. He'd sit with his mother in their basement, watching her canning. She would can the tomatoes, to use for food throughout the year. He also liked being outside, running in the fields. He greatly appreciated sharing all that time with his mother. It had been many, many years since any of that had happened. Still, when he saw flowers, this is a memory that would return to him: the two of them working in his mother's flower garden.

"It's time, my lord."

Jairoz's voice brought him back to the museum, and to the task at hand. It was time to make Rodriguez talk, or to end his life. Man tossed around the idea of turning him, but it would mean another mouth to feed. He also knew less about Rodriguez than what he knew about other humans he had turned, and that never seemed to end well. Usually, he was forced to retire them because they violated the law or lost a challenge to him. Azul was someone he had known for decades, and that certainly didn't end well either. No. Rodriguez would either talk and be released, or be eaten and destroyed.

Man knew Rodriguez was still alive. He could sense his heart beating, he could smell the beautiful stench of his blood pulsating throughout the museum. He could tell the blood type Rodriguez had. B positive. Not as delicious as other types, but it would certainly do for now. It had been days since he had drunk human blood. He and Jairoz had eaten mice during their time waiting here in the museum. At night, they would leave the grounds and search for feral cats, or birds. They found plenty, but nothing compared to the robust taste of a human's blood.

Man walked into the hall. It was filled with the most beautiful tapestries. There, at the end, he could see the outline of Rodriguez's body. He had relieved himself on the floor. He was also shivering. He was getting sick. Man knew that if he waited a few more hours, Rodriguez's blood would begin to turn sour and tasteless. This was the moment, where something had to be done.

"It's time," Man said to Rodriguez as he strolled across the museum floor. "It's time for you to help us, Mr. Rodriguez, if you value your life as much as I think you do."

Rodriguez slowly turned over on the floor. He was breathing heavily. His breaths were in and out, in and out. Man determined that while beating Rodriguez he had broken one of his ribs.

"I...I don't know who it is you want," Ben managed to blurt out.

"I want the name of the source who witnessed the subway attack," Man said. "I know you know who it is. Your deadline has arrived. Who was it that told you about it?"

"I can't remember."

Man stood over Rodriguez. He grabbed him by the stained collar of his blue button down shirt. He licked the sweat off of Rodriguez's face as he lifted him up off the ground.

"I will break you into pieces like twigs from a branch," Man said. "Don't fool with me. You got information for a story from someone you don't know? You're lying. Do you care about your life, about your wife's life? Should I bring her down here and BEAT HER TO DEATH in front of you, Mr. Rodriguez? Will that help jog your memory?"

Rodriguez burst into tears. He closed his eyes as Man tightened his grip around Ben's neck. The reporter could feel every muscle of his body tighten; he could feel the agony coursing through his veins, he could feel his life slowly draining from him.

"I..." Ben stammered weakly.

"Just say the name, Ben," Man whispered. "Tell me. So we can end this. I don't want to kill you, but I will. I swear to you I will if you make me. I will twist your body into small parts with these claws, if that's what it takes."

"I.....just..."

"WHAT? WHAT DO YOU HAVE TO SAY?" Man eased his grip on Ben's neck so he could speak more easily.

"I think you should just go fuck yourself. That's what I have to say." Ben started to chuckle slowly, as the words came out of his mouth. Then he started laughing more heavily, until it was almost maniacal. Jairoz gave him a puzzled look and exchanged glances with Man. Man tightened his grip again on Ben's neck. Ben stopped laughing as he could feel the intensified pressure on his throat.

"I want you to remember this face, Mr. Rodriguez," Man whispered. "I want you to remember the last image that you ever saw of this life." Man then squeezed Ben's neck until it nearly broke. Ben could barely breathe. His face was as blue as his shirt. Man held him there in the air for another few moments. Then he closed his eyes as unharnessed rage rose inside of him.

"What should we do my lord?" Jairoz asked.

Man let out an angry cry and bit into Rodriguez's flesh, right above the heart. Rodriguez screamed in anguish as his flesh was ripped from him. Blood spurted all over Man's face and the walls around them. Man then threw Rodriguez's body across the room. It smacked into the concrete wall, breaking into two separate pieces before dropping to the floor. Ben's guts lay all over the museum wall and floor.

"Drink of him," Man said. "Drink his blood now, Jairoz, before it is too late."

"What of you my lord? Don't you also want part of him?"

"No. I will go out tonight and find another. I don't want any part of this one."

"Yes, my lord."

"Store your strength, Jairoz. Tonight we will take vengeance on the humans for this insult. Tonight we will hunt, and gather a collection."

Jairoz smiled. "Yes, my lord." He crossed the room to feed from Rodriguez's desecrated body. Man watched, his eyes glowing with blood lust; knowing that tonight, scores of humans would be paying the same price.

20

Janine tossed and turned in bed, unable to sleep. She checked her alarm clock. It was almost 3:00 am. Her eyes burned with the pain from hustling to write all of her stories before the deadline the night before. She would have to wait at least two more hours before the daily newspaper arrived. She lay in bed, staring at the black darkness that was her bedroom ceiling. She wished she had something to help her fall asleep. She was so desperate she even tried counting sheep, which she hadn't done since she was a little girl. It didn't work. She decided to get a glass of warm milk from the kitchen.

She threw her covers off of her and sat up in bed. Then she saw him. It was the Old One, standing next to her bed. He was smiling at her, his teeth red stained with blood. She screamed. She looked down. She saw that her legs were gone. He had ripped them from her body and devoured them right next to her. And he was about to finish her off.

Janine woke up yelling. She rustled in bed violently, looking to her left and right. She stared at her alarm clock. It was almost 6:00 am. Her room was empty. Her legs were there. The vampire was not. It was an absolutely horrific nightmare.

Janine's alarm would be going off soon, so she turned it off. She sat up on the corner of her bed and unplugged her cell phone from its charger. She had received a text about an hour earlier, from Zarga. Call me ASAP, it said. Oh God. She hoped he wasn't going to be giving her any problems about her stories in the morning paper. She wore herself out writing them, and she was frankly exhausted of Zarga constantly riding her ass. If it didn't stop soon, she was going to quit the paper and move back west to see her family for awhile.

Janine called Zarga's cell. After the second ring, he answered. He sounded tired. Janine wondered when was the last time he had slept a full eight hours in a night.

"Janine, thanks for calling," he said.

She let out a sigh. "No problem. What's up?"

"I got a phone call this morning. I'm afraid I have some really bad news."

Janine's heart beat faster. "What is it?"

"Ben Rodriguez is dead."

The phone nearly dropped from Janine's hands. "What happened?"

"His wife called me just before 5. The police had contacted her. They found.....Jesus Christ. They found his head, in Inwood Hill Park in the small hours of the morning. It was floating in the river. They haven't found the rest of his body yet, but they were able to match it to his photograph somehow. Anyway, all I know right now is that he's gone, Janine. He's gone."

Janine was speechless. She was certain Ben was going to be fine. She had made a terrible mistake, not taking Painter more seriously before. This must all be true. The vampires, the link to the bite marks, all of it.

"Wait, Joe....where did you say they found him again?"

"Inwood Hill Park. Way upper Manhattan. Why, does that ring a bell?"

The Old One. She remembered he had told her to bring the human sacrifice to Inwood Hill Park. It couldn't be a coincidence. There was a connection.

"No, I just wanted to make sure I heard you right Joe. How are we going to handle this?"

"I'm going to organize a small ceremony, a remembrance service. I want to do it in the newsroom but because of the distancing guidelines and everything we will have to do it online. We'll use one of those video conferencing services. I'm going to ask people to say a few things about Ben. We'll record it and I will send the video to his wife. Would you be willing to say something?"

"Sure, Joe, that sounds nice."

"The police are investigating it as a homicide, his wife told me. We've got another fucking story to cover, and another colleague to replace. Shit. I'm so tired. I don't know how much longer I can hold the place together, Janine."

"Joe, I understand," Janine said forcefully. "You're doing all you can, everyone knows that. We'll get through this. Please, don't go to pieces. The newsroom needs you to lead us."

"Do you think this is tied to the story Ben was writing? About the subway? Could it be related to the bite attacks?"

Janine was absolutely positive that it was. She decided against telling Zarga that, until she could prove it. "I don't know. It's too soon to tell. I'll call the NYPD and see what's going on. I'll write the story too on his death if you'd like me to."

"Thanks Janine. That would be great. I appreciate it. I'll alert obits too. You can handle the murder investigation. I really do appreciate all the work you do for us. I know I bust your balls, but you're a damn good reporter. You're really going to go far. If that's what you want."

Janine paused. Not too long ago, that's exactly what she wanted. To win a Pulitzer. To own New York. To get a job working at the Times. But journalists, colleagues even, were now being killed, just for doing their job. Janine was sure of it. She couldn't prove it, but she knew in her heart Ben was murdered because of what he was writing about. He was now dead because of it. If he could be killed, then she could too.

"Thanks Joe. I'll be in as soon as I can. Talk to you soon."

Janine hung up the phone and sat in the darkness of her bedroom. She thought of Ben and his wife, whom she had met at last year's Christmas party. They shared laughs and a glass of Chardonnay together. Now the poor woman had to raise a child by herself, and she couldn't be any older than 25. Where did she work? Janine was trying to remember, but couldn't recall. She thought it was in social work, or education.

A tear formed in Janine's right eye. She could feel it slowly roll down her cheek. Then another. She stood and took a tissue out of a box on her night stand. She pressed it against her eyes as she cried, grieving for Ben and his family. She couldn't allow the newsroom to see these tears. She certainly couldn't show them to the vampire, if she saw him again. She dried her eyes and got up, turning on her bedroom light. She stared into her bedroom mirror, studying the marks the tears had left around her eyes. She looked tired. She was tired; her face was almost hanging there off the rest of her body. She closed her eyes. She thought of the vampire, and about what he said. She had to do it. She couldn't believe she was actually contemplating it, but she had to do it. She needed to forge an alliance with him. She had to get him to help her stop them. Or she too would be dead, just like Ben. Someone would find her head floating in the Hudson River.

Janine left her bedroom and went to the shower. She started to run water, waiting for it to heat up. She removed her clothes and threw them in her bathroom hamper. She grabbed her towel off the rack and lay it next to her sink. She tested the water again with her elbow and it was fine. She stepped into the shower, and released the water onto her head and neck. She

125

didn't yet know how she was going to do it, but she knew she had to. She had to find someone to bring to the park. She had to take the risk to appease the vampire, or more people would certainly die. She thought about a saying she'd heard many years ago, that one couldn't make an omelet without breaking eggs. That seemed appropriate now. As the water continued to cover her and then make its way down to the drain, Janine's mind raced over who she would get to come with her. And how the hell she would be able to get them to do it.

21

Man walked through Times Square, staring up at all the lights cascading down around him. It was totally empty, in the evening hours. This most populous spot, an easy mark to find humans for hunting, was empty. This virus was clearly affecting the city in ways he hadn't predicted. It was beautiful though, to see all of these places and not have to bump into humans, with their smells, their loud voices, their sweat. Jairoz was out collecting more humans for the feeding, but it wasn't easy. They had been out for hours, and only collected five. Three homeless, a grocery store worker, and an MTA employee.

Man took a deep breath in and stuck his nose in the air. He could feel them moving, feel them heading into their homes, feel them escaping the night air and all of its dangers. The case numbers were rising in the city, he found out in a newspaper that had been abandoned in Father Duffy square. If they wanted more numbers they would have to go to the hospitals to collect. He didn't care to do that, to risk being exposed for a few sick humans.

Man walked along west 44th street, with its large signs and advertisements. Broadway had been shut down. It would be easy to move along these streets, disguised as a homeless person. He stood in front of the entrance to the Saint James Theatre, a broadway house that had been used for many productions. This place had opened not long after Man was turned. This was where he had learned to feed, to take a human for collecting without getting caught or seen. The Old

One had taught him. You would always do it at night. A show would end. Perhaps it would be Native Son, or Oklahoma, or The King and I. The streets would fill, with tourists and theater goers, cops and beggars, looking for change. You would slowly reach out your hand and prick one on the wrist. It was best to do it to a person who was alone, and wouldn't be immediately missed in the crowd. After you had marked them, your partner would follow them and take a bite quickly on the neck. If you weren't working with a partner, you would do that yourself. Then they would be slowly turned. You could communicate to them with your thoughts. They would follow you into an alley, or even into a cab, where you could finish them. If you waited too long, they would turn into a vampire, and then you would be responsible for training them and feeding them. He learned through trial and error how long it would take to turn one.

Man walked through the theatre's stage door. Jairoz had forced it open earlier. He then made his way through the wonderful maze of dressing rooms, and storage areas, until he reached the stage itself. He looked up, into the balcony, where they were waiting. The five that were taken. They had each been marked. In another hour, they would be completely turned. This was the best time to feed. The final hour before it was too late. This was when their blood would taste best.

Jairoz was in the balcony with them. He stood and looked over onto the stage below.

"My lord, they are prepared. What shall I do?"

"Send me the first," Man replied.

Jairoz picked up an obese Caucasian woman, probably in her late 40s. Her hair was red, her skin pasty white. The grocery store worker. Jairoz threw her body over the balcony. Man caught her with his teeth; she never hit the ground. He tore into her flesh, and drank the blood from her bosom. Her breasts were large, and Man enjoyed the taste of her warm blood. He drained her completely. It took several minutes.

When it was done, Man cleaned the stage floor by licking up the remnants of her blood. "Send another," Man said.

The next was an African American man, the MTA worker. He was very young. His skin was a light caramel brown, and he was covered with acne. Man repeated the process, again and again, until all five had been drained. Jairoz jumped over the balcony when it was completed, and finished off whatever Man had left for him.

"My lord, what shall we do with the bodies," Jairoz asked.

"Leave them outside, six feet apart, along the entire street," Man replied. "It's time we sent a more powerful message to our enemies. To this corrupt and stinking city. They will think twice before spreading rumors about us in the press. We will put fear into them so they will remain silent."

"My lord, this is not enough to make a collection."

"It's enough to send the right message."

Man helped Jairoz lift the bodies and carry them out of the theatre. The street, once a place so full of life and laughter in the Times Square district, was empty. It was nearly midnight, a time when restaurants and bars would be packed with humans. A time when shows were ending and Broadway houses would close for the night. Now, there was nothing but the two of them, stacking bodies along the street in the middle of the night.

22

The newsroom was a ghost town. Janine was working at her desk, wearing a mask, and Erica was at her desk as well. No one else was around. Zarga was in his office, getting ready to call another newsroom meeting. This time, he'd have to use computer software to conference in everyone, and he was clueless about computers. She could hear him shouting over the phone to an IT employee about how to use the software. Janine hoped his bad mood wouldn't carry over into the meeting. Negativity was the last thing the newsroom needed right now.

Finally, Zarga popped his head out of his office. "Guys, come in for a meeting. Wear your masks, please," he said. Janine and Erica headed inside. Zarga was fumbling with a blue surgeon's mask, which kept slipping under his nose as he tried to speak. "I swear to God," he said, "this damn thing either slips down my face or fogs up my glasses. These are uncomfortable as hell."

"Well, we still have to wear them," Erica said.

Zarga couldn't take it anymore so he just took his glasses off. "Yes, yes, ok guys, please sit six feet apart too. I put the chairs at the right distance." Janine sat in the far corner chair and Erica took the seat next to the door. Zarga sat at his desk staring into his laptop. "Ok guys, I'm going to start this meeting. I'm on mute at the moment." He tapped some buttons on the laptop and the screen glowed.

"Ok everyone, I hope you are all safe," Zarga said. "I'm in my office with Janine and Erica, and we are the only ones at the moment working from the newsroom." Zarga went on for a few minutes about idle chat, hoping people were able to work efficiently from home.

"I have some very difficult news to share," he said. "I got word today that Ben Rodriguez is dead. He was killed." The gasps could be heard through Zarga's computer. He raised his hand to try and stop the murmurs, but it took a few minutes for all the noise to die down. "The investigation is ongoing," Zarga said. "At this time, the NYPD is investigating the case as a homicide. He was found in Inwood Hill Park." Zarga left it there. Janine was one of the few who knew the truth, that only his head was found.

"Joe, are there any leads?" Janine could make out Doug's voice.

"No, not that I'm aware of," Zarga replied. "Guys, I know this is just terrible news. It makes me sick to my stomach. But we have to put our trust in the NYPD. They are doing all they can. It's up to us to do our jobs." He put his glasses back on.

Janine knew Joe was trying to put the best light on it, but everyone was concerned. Ben was one of their own. A reporter trying to do his job; afflicting the comfortable. Her muscles tensed and she got goosebumps thinking about him. Joe was moving on, talking to Grossman about his coverage in Westchester. She zoned out of the conversation, thinking about the Old One, and what needed to be done to appease him. Who could she get to go with her to the park, late at night? She thought about using a dating app, and trying to lure an unsuspecting guy on a date with her there. Because of the virus, restaurants and bars were shut down. It would be very difficult to convince a stranger to go out with her there. There was always the chance there would be a curfew, and they could get arrested for being in a park that late at night. Her mind raced on and on, thinking about the possibilities.

"Janine?" It was Zarga, bringing her back to the present.

"Yes, sorry? I was working on something."

"What do you have cooking right now?"

"I'm working on a story about Ben. I can do a sidebar feature on him too, if you want."

"Sure. Sounds good. Let me know ASAP what you hear from the NYPD on this."

"Got it."

The meeting carried on for another 45 minutes. Zarga debriefed all the reporters, assigned stories and web posts to interns, and ran down strategy sessions with the editors. After some discussion, it was also decided to do a memorial service for Ben via computer conferencing. It would be recorded and a file of it sent to Ben's widow, as remembrance. The newsroom would also band together and buy flowers to send to

Ben's wife. After ending the meeting, Zarga asked Janine to stay behind.

"What is it Joe?"

Zarga pulled the bottle of whiskey out of his desk and poured out a glass. It was way too early to be drinking. Janine figured it was one of the only ways Joe could get through the day.

"You want any?" he asked. Janine shook her head no. He put the bottle back in his desk. "You know Janine, I remember not that long ago, we had twice as many staff. You couldn't fit everyone in our conference room. Now, we have three people working from the office and not that many more working from home. And I have to bury one of my reporters." His fingers clenched the glass as tears started to form in his eyes. "I've never had to do something like this before in 25 years in this business."

"I'm sorry Joe. I'm so sorry."

"Me too. So I'm going to ask you a question and I really need you to answer me honestly."

"OK, fine."

"Was Ben's murder committed by whoever is responsible for these bite attacks? Was it blowback for the story he wrote about them? I know you don't know for sure, but just tell me what you think."

"I think that's very possible. Probable, even. Yes."

Zarga took a long sip of his whiskey and sat back in his chair. He stared at the ceiling, studying its cracks and markings where water damage from a burst pipe had made its mark years ago.

"Janine, who is your source?"

"I can't tell you, Joe."

Zarga smacked his hand down on the desk. "Yes, Janine. Yes, you can. Because you could be next. Or me, or any one of my fucking reporters! I have to do whatever I can to protect you. And I can't do that if I am kept in the dark. So Janine, please tell me, who is your source?"

Janine's lip trembled. She wanted to tell Zarga, but didn't want him to laugh at her. She knew he wouldn't believe her if she told him the truth. She also knew that if he did believe her, that he wouldn't let her go to meet the Old One again. She stared into his eyes. He was staring right back, trying to analyze her every word. It then came to her. It was perfect. All she had to do was say it, but she couldn't. All she had to do was tell him to come with her Friday night, to meet him. She knew right then and there that he would, because he trusted her. All she had to do was get the words out, and the sacrifice would be set up. She looked away from him. She just couldn't do it. Only as a last resort, she decided.

"I'm sorry Joe, I can't tell you. Not yet, anyway. I'm still trying to figure out if this source is telling me the truth. They haven't given me anything yet that has proven to me that they're right."

Zarga angrily looked away. He opened the drawer, and slammed the whiskey bottle back onto his desk. Janine could feel the anger and pain exiting his body, filling the air. He was hurting deeply. He poured himself another glass.

"I hope you know what you're doing Janine. I didn't get a chance to warn Ben, and I should have. But I'm fucking warning you right now. This is a very dangerous game you're playing. We're all playing it, but you're in a hell of a lot deeper. You're on the radar of these people, and I can't protect you. I'm not sure anyone can at this time. I have never been the type of person to tell a reporter to stay off a story when there's heat, but I've got too much responsibility now. I'm not just a reckless reporter anymore. I have a lot to protect, including my employees. So I will ask you just this once, walk away from this. Let's go strong on virus coverage, let's do what we can with that, and just walk away from these bite stories. Sometimes you have to sacrifice your principles in order to survive." He then took another long drink.

Silence ensued. He was close to tears, staring at Janine. She couldn't look at his face, so her eyes met the floor. The silence felt like an eternity.

"I understand Joe, but I need some more time. Please. I can't do that just yet. I need to keep going for Ben's sake."

She could hear Zarga stand up and take a few steps toward the window. She could sense him trembling, trying to desperately control his anger and all the other feelings raging inside him. After clearing his throat, Zarga turned to face her.

"Then go get 'em, Janine," he said.

Janine's face broke into a slight smile. She went straight to the door and walked out.

23

Janine walked briskly to the newsroom's wall calendar. She scanned it quickly until she found what she wanted--the date of the next full moon. She had three days. Only three days, to find a sacrifice for the Old One. She went over her options as she made it back to her desk. She could join some sort of dating app--to try and lure someone to the park. That was her best bet, and it made her sick to her stomach. Was there another way? She sat at her desk staring into space when the phone rang.

It was her contact at the NYPD, Charlie Jones. He had been on the force for 20 years and now worked as a public information officer. She had a good relationship with him, he usually returned her calls before deadline. They made some small talk.

"Janine, I don't have much else to tell you right now. The investigation is ongoing."

"Please, Charlie, let me know are there any leads on what happened to Ben?"

"We think it may be tied to the bite attacks. See....we found some other bodies."

"WHAT?"

"Janine, this is just background right now. Please don't attribute this to me."

"Understood, but what happened?"

"We found five bodies, on west 44th street, early this morning. Outside the Saint James Broadway playhouse. They were mangled and...their heads were removed from the rest of their bodies."

"Oh dear God."

"The Times picked up on it first, but I haven't shared this information with them. So Janine, please tread carefully. We're cracking down on street gangs and we're going to try and set up a curfew with the mayor's office. We'll be making an announcement via webcast later today, at 3. Be on the lookout for it."

"Wow, okay. Thanks Charlie. That's really helpful. So when would this curfew go into effect?"

"I can't elaborate any more on it. Just tune in to the announcement this afternoon. We're investigating Ben's death rigorously. I can tell you, on the record, it's a top priority for us. Ben went to school with a few of the guys who are on the force. They are taking it hard."

"I'm sure they are. We are here, too. It's been just an awful few months."

"I'm sorry Janine. I'm sorry about Ben. He was very good at his job. I used to read his stuff all the time."

"Thanks Charlie. I'll talk to you soon." Janine hung up the phone and started writing. The news cycle was absolutely exploding. Every day there were more deaths. The virus was spreading throughout the city. She was completely overworked and the newsroom was understaffed. She wished Beverly was there to help her. She then got an idea. She picked up her phone and called Beverly. She answered right away.

"Hi Janine! I can't believe this about Ben!"

"I know, it's awful. How are you doing?"

"I'm fine. I'm just putting together some social media posts."

"Great. Bev, I got a tip. There's going to be an announcement today at 3, from the mayor's office, jointly with the NYPD. I want you to blast it on all our social media pages. It's in regards to the crime wave that's going on; the bite attacks."

"Okay, will do. Do you know what the announcement's going to be?"

Janine considered telling Beverly the truth but decided against it. "No," she said. "I don't. Just speculation right now. But we will find out. Oh, and Bev, thank you for all your hard work. I'm really grateful for all you're doing to help me. Are you feeling overworked?"

"No. It's been really helpful to me, all of it. I'm learning a lot. I'm really sad though about Ben, and I wish I could be there in the office with you guys."

Janine smiled. "We miss you too. Ok, so I'm writing a story about Ben, for tomorrow's paper. It's a feature piece about him. I was wondering if you would help me with it. Can you call Doug Cross and find out what his first story was, when he started here? I'm going to add that in."

"Sure. Anything else?"

"Actually yes. Just one more thing. There's a building called the Pennington. It's on the upper west side, and I was wondering if you could call over there and ask for Gregory Painter. He's one of the residents. I'll text you the number, I've got it somewhere on my desk. Call Painter and explain who you are, and see if it would be possible if I could stop by there around 5 to talk to him."

"Cool. Is that it?"

"Yes, thanks Bev. Stay safe and healthy." Janine hung up the phone and looked through her drawers. She found the number for the Pennington building. She really didn't feel like talking to Heidi, the grumpy gatekeeper. She texted the number off to Beverly and walked back over to the wall calendar. She kept staring at the date of the full moon. She wondered if this was all necessary, everything the Old One had told her. She needed to ask Painter; he had known him. Maybe this was all some sort of joke, a test like the one in the Bible with Abraham and his son. She couldn't remember much of the story, she hadn't been to church in several years. She kept telling herself this was all going to be alright. She hoped it would be alright. That it would never actually have to happen. Still, she had to prepare for the worst.

Her desk phone rang again. She ran over and looked at the caller ID. It was Doug Cross. He probably wanted to give her the background on Ben's history. She answered. Doug's voice sounded anxious.

"Janine, hey. How are you? This is just terrible news about Ben."

"Yes, I know. I'm working on a story about him, a feature."

"Yeah, Bev just called me. I told her I would tell you everything you needed to know."

"Thanks Doug. So when did he start working here?"

"Three years ago. I remember it was in the fall, he was hired as a general assignment reporter, but Joe put him on city hall coverage, and on legislative news in Albany when the session was going on."

"Thanks Doug. That's great to know. I will definitely include that."

"And his first story was actually about a piece of legislation passed by the city council. The City Business Transparency Act. It mandated that all public meetings in the city hall building be broadcast online. City Council, Buildings Commission, everything. Nothing really sexy, but I remember it was good copy when it came out. Only a few news outlets had a full-time city hall reporter."

"Okay, thanks Doug. I will make a note of it."

"Great. Anything else?"

"I don't think so. So, I'll..."

"Janine," Doug interrupted, "how are you doing? I mean, in light of absolutely everything that's going on."

Janine sighed. She didn't try and think about it. "I'm doing alright. Staying busy. My hands are really full at the moment. And I don't have access to my intern in the newsroom, so we have to talk all the time by phone. How about you?"

"It's been difficult. Most of our news morgue isn't backed up on computer files yet, so I don't have access to lots and lots of stuff that I'd like."

"I understand. Listen, I--"

"Janine, listen, I know things are really difficult right now, and I know that you don't know too many people in New York. I was wondering if Friday night, you would want to get some dinner with me? We can't go out to a restaurant of course but we could make some type of arrangement that's comfortable for you."

"Wait Doug, aren't you married?"

He had a quick answer to that. "I'm getting divorced, remember?"

Janine was shocked. Doug was about 15 years older than her and had never shown any interest in her before. Maybe he had romantic feelings; maybe he was just doing it to be nice. Janine thought about the date he had given her. Friday. It was the night of the full moon. She had an opening.

"Listen, Doug, I am really flattered. Let me think about it; things are pretty busy now. May I call you back later today?"

"Of course! Hopefully it works out. I make a mean plate of pasta."

"That sounds nice. I'll call you back later today, okay? Thanks, Doug, it's really sweet of you.:"

Janine hung up the phone. She couldn't believe that Doug had asked her out. He was actually kind of a boring person, but he didn't seem to be too bad of a guy. She mulled over his offer while working on her story. Her phone rang yet again. Damn, she thought, I'm popular today.

It was Zarga. "Janine," he said, "I got an email from Beverly with posts to edit about an announcement today. What's going on?"

"Sorry Joe, I've been on the phone. Yes. There's a joint announcement coming from the mayor's office and the NYPD today at 3. Off the record, it looks like they're going to announce a curfew because of the bite mark attacks. They found more victims."

"The Times has that, yes. Can we confirm?"

"I did. Five bodies found on west 44th street in the theatre district. Right in Times Square."

"Oh God. Jesus, this story is just getting worse and worse. Okay, I will edit Beverly's stuff and we'll put it on the web. Can you cover the announcement?"

"Yeah. I'll find out if I can get down there."

"No, don't worry about that. I don't want to risk you being out, with the virus and these maniacs on the loose. I'll feel better with you working from the newsroom. Just get the webcast. How are we moving with Ben's story?"

"I got some good info for the feature piece. His beginnings at the paper, working on city hall coverage. As for the homicide investigation, the NYPD is basically just giving me a stock response right now."

"Damn. OK." He let out a long sigh over the phone. "I want you to quote me in your feature. This. He was a hard-working, kind hearted man, and I know he'll be greatly missed by every single person in our newsroom."

"Thanks Joe."

"And if you can Janine...."

"What?"

"Could you leave out the anecdotes about him and me drinking alcohol in the break room?"

Janine smiled. "Will do."

"OK. A few TV stations are interviewing me too; they're covering his death. Would you be willing to sit in and do these interviews with me? It's all happening via computer. The first one's in 10 minutes. Could you swing by the office?"

Janine really didn't want to be interviewed. She wasn't as close to Ben as Joe or even Howard Grossman was. Grossman was in Westchester, so she guessed she was the best alternative to fill in.

"Sure Joe. Give me ten. I'll be there."

Janine's phone buzzed. She saw another call was coming in. It might be the NYPD, she thought, with more information about Ben. She switched over. It was Beverly.

"Hi Janine, I sent my stuff for today over to Joe."

"Sounds great. Thanks Bev."

"I called the Pennington, too. I tried to talk to Gregory Painter."

"Tried to?"

"He's been hospitalized. I'm so sorry Janine. Apparently, he has the virus."

"What? Who did you speak to?"

"Their receptionist, a woman named Heidi Bl--"

"I know her. Did she say anything else?"

"Apparently there's been an outbreak in that building."

"You better call Erica and tell her. She can write a story."

"Janine, are you okay?"

Janine paused. No, she was not okay. Not by any stretch of the imagination. She just wanted to explode. She wanted to tell Beverly everything: about the vampire at 91st street, about Painter and his rantings, about how she had to play a part in a human sacrifice. She wanted to just blurt it all out there so it was out in the open.

"I'm okay. Thanks Bev. Thanks for calling too. Did she say anything else about his condition? Or where they were taking him?"

"Sisters of Mercy hospital in the Bronx. I don't know about his condition. Hospitals are filling up with patients."

"I know. Thanks Bev. I really appreciate it. I have to go. Some TV news people are interviewing Joe and me about Ben. They're about to call us."

"Oh wow. Let me know which ones! I'll be sure to tune in. It's so sad that he's gone. He was a really nice guy."

"Bye Bev."

Janine sat at her desk, processing what Beverly just told her. She had to talk to Painter, before Friday's full moon. She had to determine whether this was all real. She got up and walked to Zarga's office, knocking on the door.

"Come in."

Janine pushed her head in. "Joe, I'm sorry but something's come up. I've got to follow up on something for this story about Ben. Is it okay if I don't do the interviews with you? I'll only be gone an hour."

Zarga frowned and got up from his desk. "Janine, are you sure? I don't feel comfortable with you out there. Can you just give me 30 minutes here; then I'll go with you."

Janine was shocked. Joe wanted to hold her hand? She understood that times were dangerous, but it was in the middle of the day and she knew how to take care of herself. Plus, she didn't know for certain but she had a hunch the Old One was keeping tabs on her, somehow. She could feel him in the air, not far from her. The hairs on her neck began to stand up.

"Joe, I will be fine. I just need an hour, maybe two at the most. I will be back for the mayor's announcement at 3."

"Okay, please keep your phone on at all times. I'm a phone call away."

"I understand. Thanks Joe. Will be back soon."

Janine looked at her phone. It was almost 1. She had just over two hours to make it back to the newsroom. The hospital was about 40 minutes on the subway, so that didn't leave her much time. She'd have to do a rideshare or hail a cab. Lots of ride share services were shutting down, so it could be difficult. She quickly checked her phone again, to see how often the subway was running. A train would be coming into the nearest station in four minutes! She could make that train if she hauled ass. She quickly grabbed a few things from her desk and raced out of the newsroom. She could hear Erica yelling at her as she ran. She didn't have time to gossip, she had to get to the station.

On the street, it was eerily silent. There was no one around Janine, as she wrapped her mask around her face. Thankfully she didn't wear glasses, or they would be constantly fogged up from the mask. She sprinted down 42nd street until she got to 8th avenue. This normally crowded space, filled with people coming and going from the Port Authority Bus Terminal, was almost empty. She ran down the subway steps, and swiped her fare card. It didn't go through. She was in a spot where no agent was around to help her. She cursed under her breath. She tried again, and this time it went through. She ran through the gate and kept hustling as she neared the uptown platform. She could hear a train moving into the station. Janine nearly tripped down the steps as she kept pushing forward, toward the sliding doors of the train. She slipped in, just as it was about to close its doors to the 42nd street platform. Lady luck was on her side.

***

Sisters of Mercy Hospital was filled to the brim with people screaming, yelling, and wearing masks. There were two buses outside the front doors. They had brought in nurses from New Jersey and Connecticut to help with the influx of virus patients. A tent was set up outside as well, with a long line of people waiting to get in. Janine walked up to a nurse who was standing near the entrance.

"What's going on here?" Janine pointed her finger at the tent.

"It's a testing area. People are getting tested to see if they have the virus. The sickest ones get a room, the others get sent home with some aspirin," the nurse replied. She was a young girl, either from China or Taiwan, Janine guessed. Janine had visited both countries while an undergraduate student in Arizona. Janine wished she had scrubs with her, to impersonate one of the nurses so she could get inside. She'd have to lie to force her way into the hospital, if necessary, to find Painter. A life was at stake.

"Do you need help with something? I'm Grace," the nurse said.

"Yes. Thanks. My father's been taken here, and I don't know where he is."

"I'm sorry. Do you see him in the line?"

150

"No, he's inside. He's gotten the virus. I think he's been given a room, but I don't know for sure. I need to get inside."

"I'm sorry but it's too dangerous. Especially if you aren't feeling symptoms. You could contract the virus."

"Please! His name's Gregory and no one is in there with him!" Janine tried as hard as she could to muster some tears.

"I'm sorry, I really am. Believe me, I don't want to make things worse for you. Maybe I can check and see on his condition for you."

"Oh could you please! Thank you Grace, thank you so much."

Grace smiled at her. "No problem, wait here, Miss....

"Painter. I'm Janine. He's Gregory, my dad. Gregory Painter." Janine grimaced as she lied right through her teeth to this sweet young nurse. Grace nodded her head and walked into the hospital.

Janine's mind raced. She had to find a way inside, no matter the cost. She had to speak to Painter about the Old One. She looked to her right as a group of people were arguing with a security guard about getting inside. Janine looked at the entrance. The door was guarded by two other security guards. They looked armed to the teeth. Janine frowned. She had to be back by 3. She looked at her phone. It was almost 2. She ran the numbers in her head. She had 25 minutes to get inside, speak with Painter, and run to the train. The subway was stopping here every 10 minutes. If she missed the 2:20 train, she wouldn't make it back to work on time. And if Grace didn't help her, she would lose valuable time trying to find Painter in this maze of a hospital.

A few minutes passed. Janine broke into a sweat, as she anxiously kept looking at her phone. Too much time was getting away from her. She started toward the front door when finally Grace walked through the doors.

"Hi! Sorry for the wait. I have some bad news."

"What?" Janine feared the worst.

"Well, your father is going to have to be put on a ventilator. He is having a lot of trouble breathing. We are short on ventilators at the moment. We are getting a shipment in, but until then we can just make him comfortable."

Janine played the part of a distraught daughter to the best of her ability. "So what does that mean? Is he dying? WHERE IS HE?"

Grace put her hand on Janine's shoulder. "He's getting treatment. He's in with some other patients who are also waiting for ventilators. They're on the third floor. I assure you, we are doing everything we can. I'm so sorry. I know how hard this is. We are all working as hard as we can for the patients." Janine could see a tear forming in Grace's eye. She looked sad, almost defeated. Janine bet she hadn't slept in awhile. Janine decided to tone down the attitude a bit.

"I'm sorry Grace, I know you are. But please, let me see him. It's an absolute emergency."

"I'm sorry...." Just then, the group of people arguing rushed the doors. The security guard tried to restrain them but they threw their arms at him. Janine pulled Grace out of the way, as the two other security guards rushed forward. It looked like an awkward dance, as the angry mob grappled with the security officers. Janine forcefully pushed Grace away, as she saw for a split second, a clear path to the front door. It was now or never. Janine decided then and there, to go for it. She rushed to the door. Grace screamed at her. Janine just kept running, it didn't matter what happened now. She had to get to the third floor. She had to find Painter.

Janine passed through the front doors, panting for breath. "THEY ARE FIGHTING OUTSIDE! HURRY! GET SECURITY DOWN HERE!" She screamed at the other hospital personnel in the lobby. Nurses and another security guard rushed out to add to the confusion, as they created a log jam right at the door. No one could get in and no one was getting out. Good, Janine thought. It worked. Grace wouldn't be able to get to her, at least for a few more minutes.

Janine ran to the end of the hallway to where the stairs were. She pushed her weary body up two more floors. She didn't see anyone on the staircase. The commotion outside sounded more and more violent.

153

She hoped no one was hurt. Finally, she came to a large white door with a huge 3 painted on it in black lettering. She had made it. She looked through the glass, to see if anyone was near the door. She could see nurses moving to and fro, and a few people in beds positioned in the hallway. She adjusted her mask. She needed to be careful, she kept telling herself. These people had the virus.

She opened the door and slipped into the hallway. The nurses couldn't see her. She tiptoed to the first door she could find and went in. A hospital patient room. Three patients were in a room built for two. She saw that all three had ventilators. They wouldn't have been Painter. She slipped back out the door and rushed to the room across the hall. Again, a patient room for two. There were four patients inside this time.

"NURSE! Move Mr. Painter to the room across the hall!" She could hear someone yelling it from the hallway. Then, footsteps. They were heading in her direction. Someone was coming to her room. As soon as the steps reached the doorway, they stopped. Janine quickly hid in the room's bathroom, out of sight. She swung the door until it was nearly closed. She left it open just a touch so she could hear if someone was entering the room. Two nurses came in. Janine held her breath as they moved past the bathroom door and over to one of the beds. This was possibly Painter, she thought. The nurses began moving the bed as Janine crouched down in the bathroom. These patients didn't have ventilators, and

154

the ones did across the hall. They were probably going to put him on one of them. She could hear the nurses talking to each other as they rolled the bed toward the door.

"Mr. Painter here needs to be on a ventilator. Easy! Watch the wall there," one of the nurses said. She sounded like she was in charge.

"We're giving him one?" the other one asked.

"We're going to have to share. He's going to go on the one with Mr. Rohel across the hall, until we get our new shipment in. This is just terrible. We need about 50 more of these damn ventilators," the first nurse said.

Janine just waited as patiently as she could while the nurses pushed the bed out of the room. She could hear them complaining about a shortage of orderlies. Janine checked her phone. It was a minute past two. She was losing time. She texted Zarga, letting him know she may be a few minutes late to the office but would still be able to get everything done before the deadline. Zarga texted back an angry face and asked what was going on. She ignored it. Janine rested with her back against the bathroom door. She started breathing deeply; in and out, in and out. She could then hear yelling in the hallway. Janine raised her head to listen intently as doctors, nurses and orderlies were shouting about the commotion outside. They were going to have to lock the hallway doors to keep people from getting in. Janine started cursing again under her breath. She had to get moving, even if that meant risking being seen. She stood up and pushed herself slowly out of the bathroom. She popped her head into the hallway. Orderlies and nurses were running all over, rolling patients' beds into rooms and checking doors. Janine glanced quickly into the room across the hall. She could see the nurses working. They must have been trying to get Painter hooked up to the ventilator. She had to distract them, to get them to stop somehow. She saw their room number next to the door and got an idea.

"NURSES IN ROOM 305! Please help us get these patients out of the hallway and into Room 312!" Janine yelled at them and then quickly hid back behind the door. The nurses snapped to attention and walked into the hallway. They looked in both directions.

"Did you hear that? Who said it?" The senior nurse asked. The young girl didn't say anything. "OK, let's go," the senior nurse said as she hustled down the hall toward a patient's bed in the hallway. The younger nurse followed her. Janine sprinted across the hall into room 305 and quickly closed the door. She locked it behind her. It was her only chance to get to speak with Painter. She wasn't even sure this patient was actually him, but she had to take the risk. Somehow, everything up to that point had worked out miraculously.

Janine looked at the patient in the bed. It was Painter, but she could barely recognize him. He was very frail and weak. He was asleep. He still wore his wire rim glasses, and his thinning white hair was unkempt. She was taken aback by how much his physical appearance had changed in that short amount of time. Still, she needed to speak with him. She carefully nudged him on the shoulder. He didn't stir.

"Gregory," Janine whispered. Quietly at first, and then louder. "Mr. Painter, please wake up."

Painter stirred. He slowly opened his eyes and turned his head toward Janine. His blue eyes had sleep crust around them and appeared bloodshot. Janine whispered and gently nudged him again.

"What is it," Painter finally grunted. His voice was very hoarse and raspy. He looked at Janine. "Oh, I know you, don't I?"

"It's Janine Gomes, sir. The reporter for the Daily Reporter."

"Yes, yes." He then coughed. Janine took a step back from him and tightened her mask around her face. She was starting to feel afraid for the first time since she'd broken into the hospital.

"Mr. Painter, I'm sorry to bother you, but I need to speak with you. It's urgent. I......I took your advice. I went to the station."

"What station?"

Janine frowned. Painter must have been heavily sedated. He didn't seem to remember who she was or anything he had told her. Janine was nearly out of time, and this really wasn't going well at all for her.

"Mr. Painter, you told me about...about your friend at the station. The abandoned station at 91st street." She leaned over to him as close as she could, so the other patients wouldn't hear her. They probably couldn't hear, anyway. "You told me about who lived there. The vampire. The....Old One."

Painter's eyes widened. He gripped the bed sheets tightly with his wrinkled hands. He turned his head away from Janine and stared at the wall.

"I.....I...don't think I...know who you're talking about."

"Please, please! Mr. Painter, please I can't afford to play games. I went there. I went to 91st street. I met him. I saw him. The Old One. He....remembered you." As Janine spoke, Painter started to make small grunting noises. They were very quiet at first and then started to get louder and louder. He began to toss around in the bed.

"No....no....," he said. He looked and sounded just terrible. Janine could hear voices in the hall. She had to keep the conversation moving.

"Mr. Painter, I need to ask you something. The Old One told me about something I needed to do for him. A...sacrifice. I needed to bring him someone, to...sacrifice. In order for him to trust me. In order for him to help me, he needed me to do this for him."

"Not me, not me, no...."

"No Mr. Painter, I didn't mean you. I have to ask, is this true? The Old One, is he telling me the truth do you think? Or is he lying? Can I trust him to keep his word?"

"I....." Painter started coughing again. A deep cough that seemed to come from his chest. It kept on and on. Janine realized it was over. She wouldn't be able to get anything from him. This man was dying. The virus and whatever else ailed him were ripping apart the insides of his body. Janine stood there next to his bed, hoping the cough would stop. It wasn't. She rushed to the bathroom and got him a glass of water. She came back to his bed and handed him the glass. His hands shook as he reached out for it. Janine took his hand and helped him grip it. She assisted him in getting the glass to his lips. Janine apologized to Painter for bothering him. He drained the water from the glass, his hands shaking. Janine truly felt sorry for him. He was going to die in this hospital room. He was going to die all by himself. This was a man who dedicated his life to the people of New York, to getting them the information and news that mattered to them. Now, none of that work mattered. He was going to die---alone, and unappreciated.

Janine re-filled his glass. She helped him grip it and then drink it again. Painter was having some trouble breathing, but was able to reach out and grab her hand. The voices in the hall were louder, and sounded closer.

"Th...thank you," Painter said. He gave her hand a light squeeze and went back to drinking.

Janine watched him finish it. She checked her phone. It was 2:15. She had to go. Her mission to the hospital had been a failure. Now she had to figure out a way out of here without being seen. Painter closed his eyes and looked like he was about to nod off again. She squeezed his hand one last time. She pulled his blanket back up to his chin. She took one last look at his hangdog face, and then turned away from him and unlocked the door.

***

Janine retraced her steps and made it back down to the main floor. There were police officers and hospital personnel all over the lobby. The aftermath of the scuffle. She kept an eye out for Grace but didn't see her. She took out her reporter's notebook, in case she had to come up with some alibi. It turned out that she would need it. A police officer stopped her in the lobby.

"Miss, what are you doing here? Who are you?"

"Janine Gomes, reporter for the Daily Reporter. I got a call that there had been a fight here and a bunch of people were trying to storm into the hospital. Do you know what's been going on?"

"No comment, ma'am. I'm going to have to ask you to leave. You can't be in here. We're cleaning out the lobby now. Hospital personnel only."

"OK, fine. Understood officer. I'll wait outside and find out who to speak with."

The ruse worked. The cop didn't press the issue and Janine quickly walked out. The entrance was filled with people in masks, moving all around. The police had a few people sitting on the curb in handcuffs. She recognized two of them. They had been arguing with the security guards when Janine went in. She turned her head and walked away so they wouldn't recognize her. Janine pulled out her phone and checked the time. 2:25. She would make the 2:30 train, and be back in the newsroom a few minutes after 3. She texted Zarga to let him know. She then pulled up her contacts list and scrolled until she found the number she was looking for. She made the call and it went straight to voicemail.

"Hi, Doug. It's Janine. Sorry I couldn't give you an answer earlier. Friday night sounds great. Why don't we meet near my place? I'll text you the address."

24

The collection had begun. Man and Jairoz spent several consecutive nights collecting bodies all over the city. In every borough, they could find someone out when they shouldn't be. They collected young and old, rich and poor, sick and well. Man could smell the virus on a few of them, but decided to keep them. They wouldn't be eaten, but they would be kept. They would be caged, like pets, for his approval and pleasure.

At the museum they stored the bodies. Some were young and quite beautiful, others older and more wrinkled. Obese, even. Man and Jairoz wouldn't usually eat someone who was obese, the fat stifled out the taste of the blood. This time, he didn't mind. Man and Jairoz were the last two vampires left in the city. They were the last of their kind. Man decided not to turn any of the humans they had collected. They would all be his pets. They would find food for him. They would serve him. He wasn't worried about getting caught. He wasn't worried about these pitiful humans seeking revenge against him. The humans were weak, divided and disorganized. They hated each other over politics, sex, wealth. Man knew their strengths; knew their weaknesses. He had lived among them for so long.

Jairoz would collect from lower Manhattan, and Brooklyn each night. He would bring back humans, but also news and information for Man. Jairoz would collect newspapers and cell phones, devices that could be used to store information and communicate with the humans. Jairoz also stored issues of the New York Daily Reporter newspaper to see if they were able to discover who had killed Ben Rodriguez. One night, he presented an issue of the paper to Man.

"My lord, more stories here about the attacks," Jairoz said.

"This human is very intelligent, her perseverance is admirable," Man replied after studying it.

"She keeps writing about the bite attacks. She seems to know more than most others about us."

"We retired her colleague. That should be enough to let her know to stay away from us. She has no idea of knowing where we are, anyway."

"I think we should take care of her, my lord. She's the only person I can see writing in these newspapers that's talking about the attacks every day."

"We could, yes. But wouldn't that draw more attention to what we're doing? We took care of one reporter. One reporter's death could be a freak accident, a random murder. To take care of two, that would reveal a larger pattern. That would bring us too much attention."

"What if she finds out where we are? You've seen her work. She's not stupid. She could find us."

"She won't. No one human is cunning enough to discover a vampire's den. Unless..."

"Unless what my lord?"

"Unless she is brought here by someone who knows where it is."

"Who knows where we are?"

"Just you and I, Jairoz. You've never met this woman, have you?"

"No my lord. Of course not."

"Then she won't find us." Man looked at the newspaper again. He re-read the article that Janine had written. "She is very, very intelligent though, isn't she?"

"She knows great details about what marks we leave on the bodies."

Man put down the newspaper. He put his claws behind his back and paced the museum floor. He stroked his face, lost in thought. He pondered what could be done. True, this writer did know details about what they did to the bodies. But she didn't know their true nature; she didn't know that they were vampires. Man walked by the humans that he and Jairoz had caged. He stared into their vacant eyes, as he paced the floor.

"Jairoz, how many humans have we collected in total?"

"10, my lord."

"Two of them have this virus. I smell it in their blood."

"I understand."

"Release these two. Have them follow this writer. Have them report back to you each night on her whereabouts. Have them find out where she goes, what she does. Who she meets with. Then you report it back to me. If she gets too close to us, then we will take care of her."

"Yes, my lord."

Jairoz drank from the two. He spit out their blood, as it was contaminated from the virus. Then, in the ancient language, he repeated the orders Man had given him. The two humans, a man and woman in their 40s who had been married, repeated the orders back to Jairoz. They then left the museum, to start their mission. Man watched them go. He smiled. He was pleased with all that had been, and all that was about to be done.

25

Janine met Doug Cross on Friday night near Inwood Hill Park. It was a clear and chilly evening. She lied to him, and felt lousy about it. She said she lived near there. Since restaurants were closed, they got take out food and ate it in the park. He wanted Chinese, but there wasn't any available. They settled on Thai instead. Janine took mental notes of as much of the park as she could, looking over her shoulder trying to see if the Old One was there. She couldn't see him, but she did feel as if someone or something was observing them.

Janine then suggested they take a long walk, to digest the food and get to know each other. They headed up Broadway, walking toward the Bronx. Janine didn't really like Doug after talking to him. He made inappropriate comments, bragged a lot about himself, and didn't even offer to pay for her meal. She guessed she was a little old-fashioned that way.

Doug did however talk a lot about the history of the paper, and Janine was somewhat interested in it. Doug knew a lot of history about the city as well. Janine decided to probe him for some information as they crossed over the Harlem East river.

"So do you know much about the mole people? I know that they were at the abandoned station at 91st street," Janine said to him.

"Yes. In the 80s, it was really bad, there were hundreds of people living in the subways. They usually took over the abandoned stations. In the 90s the mayor started to break them up and get rid of them."

"Where did they go?"

"They were forced out of town. They were put on buses and driven out of the city. Some I'm sure came back, but the MTA worked very aggressively to keep people out of the tunnels. It's been that way ever since."

"You said they lived in the abandoned stations?"

"Yeah. Some lived on platforms too, or on the actual trains."

"So how many abandoned stations are there?"

Doug laughed. "Oh several. There are three or four in Manhattan. Several others in Brooklyn too. The transit museum in Brooklyn is located in one. I think the museum runs tours of some of them."

"Where are the ones in Manhattan?"

Doug scratched his head. "I know there's the one at 91st, then there's a few on the east side. I think there's one actually underneath the Waldorf Astoria Hotel. But the crown jewel is at City Hall."

Janine's face lit up. "Wait! I have heard about that one! It's underneath city hall and it has all the chandeliers and brick walls?"

"Yes. It was the first station ever built. They closed it 50 years ago or something like that. It's really pretty. I've seen pictures online."

"Wow. It would be great to go there."

Doug looked at his watch and stopped. "Janine, it's getting late. I think the curfew is at 11. We should be heading back."

"What time is it now?"

"10:15."

Janine frowned. She had nearly two hours to go, just to get Doug to the rock. As they turned and walked back toward Manhattan, Janine started to panic. How could she do this? Doug was a bore, but he wasn't a bad man. In fact, if she were older she may have been happy to be with him. He certainly was intelligent, but so tedious. A cold breeze blew as they walked off the bridge. Janine shivered. Doug tried putting his arm around her, but stopped. Janine stopped and turned to him.

"Why did you stop?" she said.

"I'm sorry. I just thought you looked cold and wanted to try to warm you up."

"It's okay. I don't mind."

Doug put his arm around her and walked beside her. The cold wind blew even more strongly, reaching into her bones with its cold grasp. Janine started to cry. All the emotion, all the stress, all the anguish of the last few weeks was hitting her at once. She didn't want Doug to die. Sure, he was probably just being nice because he wanted to sleep with her, but that didn't justify what she was about to do. Janine froze. She turned away from Doug. She didn't want to go through with this. She rubbed her eyes and ran her hands through her hair. There just had to be another way.

"Janine, are you okay? What's wrong?" Doug asked.

"Doug. I'm sorry. I....."

"What is it?"

Janine turned back to him, with a tear stained face. "Doug, if you could do something, to help stop all this madness, to help protect millions of innocent people. Would you do it? Even if it meant risking your own life?"

Doug stared at her. There was a long silence.

"What do you mean Janine?"

"Would you be willing to sacrifice your life if it meant saving the lives of many others?"

Doug smiled. "Wow, that's a first for me. I usually don't get asked that question on a first date."

Janine laughed. It was a big beautiful belly laugh. She couldn't remember the last time she laughed so hard. It wasn't even that what Doug said was funny. It was just unexpected. It was also needed to cut all the tension she had dwelling deep inside of her. Doug's smile faded.

"Jesus, Janine, is it really that funny to think that this is a date? Are you embarrassed by me?"

"No, please Doug, don't be upset. I'm sorry."

"That was just not very nice of you." Doug walked away in silence. He was sulking, Janine could tell. She wanted to just go home. She checked her phone. It was nearly 11. The curfew would be at 11. She had to keep Doug out here another hour. He was making it easier for her with his pissy attitude.

"Doug, don't go," she said.

He turned to face her. His face was red. So were his ears. Great, she thought. She was going to have to turn on her charm to win him over again. She didn't want to have to play games, but it just felt like it was inevitable.

"Janine, it's late. I had a good time tonight, but I think it's time to get home. The curfew is starting soon."

"Let's just stay out a little longer. I don't want the evening to end on a low note."

"Janine, it's..."

"Oh JESUS! FINE! I'm sorry Doug, I thought you had a good sense of adventure to you. I thought you were a cool guy. I thought you weren't just another bore wandering around the office. That's why I agreed to this date. But I think I was wrong about you.

You're just another play it by the book, risk nothing, boring person."

She had pushed in her chips. She was gambling on Doug not wanting to be a bore, that he would try to prove her wrong. She gave him a cold stare as she walked away from him. She started walking briskly, hearing nothing behind her. Her face crinkled with worry. It didn't seem like her gamble had worked. Then finally, Doug started running back toward her.

"Janine, wait!" he yelled.

Janine smiled as she turned back to face him. "What?"

"You're right, Janine, I am a cool guy. I'm sorry that I got upset. It was just a weird question, I guess. Anyway, I agree. Let's not let the evening slip away like this."

Janine smiled at him. "Good."

"But we gotta keep away from the cops. The main streets probably aren't a good idea. Also, the subway may be off limits for awhile."

"Let's take a walk in the park."

"Central Park? That's like 60 blocks from here."

"No silly, there's one near here. Inwood Hill Park."

"Oh. Yeah, I think we were walking by there earlier. But is it safe this late at night?"

"Come on, don't be a bore Doug."

Doug frowned. "Okay, okay. You lead the way."

Janine started walking west toward the park. It was about six blocks away she figured. She took a long gulp. After days and days of waiting, it was finally here. She had done it. She'd convinced Doug Cross to go to Inwood Hill Park with her, to face the Old One. If he was telling the truth, that is. A pit seemed to form in Janine's stomach as she led Doug on. Her stomach started to ache from the stress that was taking over her body. Her throat was dry. She had no idea what to expect. If no one showed up, she could try and just enjoy the rest of her evening with Doug. If this thing did show up, and was lying to her, maybe she and Doug could find a way to get away from him. How did you destroy a vampire again? She tried to remember. Crosses. Garlic. Sunlight. She didn't have any of those things with her. She doubted that Doug did, either.

The two walked in silence. It was after 11 now. The curfew had started. Two police cars were patrolling the streets in the neighborhood. Janine and Doug slipped into alleys and doorways to avoid them as best they could. Finally, Janine saw the entrance to the park.

"Wow, it looks creepy doesn't it?" Doug asked.

Janine laughed nervously. "We'll be fine. What, are you afraid? Think we'll run into a vampire or something?"

"Vampires? Don't be ridiculous."

The couple walked through the entrance. To the right was a baseball diamond, to the left were some benches and restrooms. There was a man dressed in rags asleep on one of the benches. Janine froze while looking at him. She couldn't see his face. She grabbed Doug's arm as they passed him.

"Don't worry, he won't bother us," Doug said.

Janine smiled at him as they walked deeper into the park. Janine kept an eye out for the rock the Old One told her about, but couldn't find it. It was just too dark. They strolled around the baseball diamond, when Doug stopped to face her.

"Janine, listen. I really like you. I like spending time with you. But I have to ask, why did you bring me here?"

Janine was lost for words. Her mind started racing for excuses. She absolutely had to get him to the rock by midnight. Then, an idea finally came to her.

"Okay, Doug, this is silly, but there's a spot here in the park I have always wanted to see. Supposedly, there's a ghost story about it."

Doug's ears perked up. "Oh really? What is it?"

"There's a rock here in the park. It's a sacred rock. If you go there at midnight, you are supposed to be met by the ghost of an old man. Then, you will be blessed with a wish."

Doug laughed. "You mean like the Aladdin genie? I think you're sweet Janine, but that just sounds silly."

Janine playfully pushed him in the arm. "Shut up, buster. Would you just find it with me? I think it would be fun. Supposedly, once you meet the ghost, he asks you a question. You have to answer it correctly to get your one wish. Or, you could give him a gift. I brought something, that we can use as a gift!"

Doug looked at her with interest. "Okay, what is it?"

Janine put her finger to her lips. "Shh....it's a secret. We have to see the ghost first."

It had worked. Doug agreed to help her find the rock. Janine looked at her phone. 11:45. They only had 15 minutes! Janine had remembered at the park entrance there was a map. She took Doug by the hand and led him back to the entrance. She had to use her phone as a flashlight to see the map in the dark. Her fingers scrolled over the map till she finally found what she was looking for--Shorakkopoch Rock.

It wasn't too far from where they were. She figured they could make it there in about seven minutes. That should get them at the rock just before midnight. The moon glared brightly in the sky as they made their way to the rock. It was a long gravel trail that winded around a beautiful green space. There were a few people sleeping in the park. Janine and Doug tried their best not to get too close to them.

Janine worked up a sweat power walking to the rock. Doug could barely keep up with her. He complained a few times about how fast she was walking, but shut up after she reminded him about the time.

Finally, they made it. She could see the outline of the rock glowing in the moonlight. It was a large gray stone, surrounded by dirt. It stuck out in the park like a sore thumb. She was in awe of this beautiful piece of nature, and curious about what powers it may hold. She couldn't stop thinking about the Old One, and if what he had said was true.

Doug walked around to the front of the rock. There was a plaque on it. It was dark brown with gold lettering. It talked about a tree that had stood there for centuries, one of the links to the Native American tribes and people that had once lived in the area. It also stated that the rock was the site where the Native Americans had sold Manhattan Island to the white men. It was paid for with trinkets and beads, it said. Doug and Janine exchanged glances in the dark as they read about the history of the place.

Doug rubbed his hands together. "Okay, so we're here. What do we do now? Do you have the gift?"

Janine looked at him. She was about to speak, but realized she wasn't sure what to do. The Old One had said to bring someone there at midnight. She checked her phone. One minute to midnight!

"Let's wait here for a few minutes," she said. "The ghost is supposed to appear here and meet you."

Doug nodded his head. He looked around. It was pitch black. "Okay Janine, I think this is just silly, but if you want to stay, that's fine. I'm not going to leave you here alone. Jesus this is creepy."

"I know. Wait, did you hear that?"

There was a rustling sound. It was coming from the woods behind the rock. There were leaves, crunching. Janine reached out for Doug and held his hand. She could barely make it out. A figure. It was standing about 10 feet from them. Janine tried to shine her phone flashlight on it, but she dropped her phone in the dirt. As she was picking it up, the figure spoke. It was the voice of the Old One.

"You have come. This is your sacrifice?" His voice didn't hiss like it had in the subway tunnel. It sounded clearer and richer again. Janine trembled.

"I...I thought you were joking," she said. Then, a pause. "But I wanted to make sure."

Doug chimed in. "Janine, what are you talking about? Who is this?"

"You didn't tell him," the Old One whispered.

"Who the fuck are you?" Doug said. He was shaking. He took a step back. Janine held on to his arm, but Doug tried to squirm away. Janine's fingers dug into his arm. She had to keep him there. It was her conscience telling her; her natural reaction. She realized then and there that everything she had heard from the Old One was true. Slowly, it walked towards them. Doug was nearly away from her. She dug deeper with her hands, until she could hear him groan in pain. It felt like blood was seeping from his arm. Suddenly, the Old One was on him. He had sunk his teeth into Doug's arm. Janine let go in horror. She staggered back, watching the Old One drink from Doug's arm. Doug screamed for help. Janine froze. She couldn't do anything to stop what was coming. She had come too far. She had hoped it was all a joke, or some type of test. It wasn't. It was all very real.

In an instant, Doug passed out. The Old One twisted and broke his arm as Doug's body slid to the ground. Janine watched as the Old One carried his body to the rock. The vampire held onto the rock with his right hand as he had Doug's body in his left. He lifted Doug up and leaned him against the rock. Janine watched each step. Blood trickled onto the rock. The Old One started speaking in another language. It sounded terrifying. It sounded like some sort of prayer. He had his head bowed. He was kneeling on the ground. She was transfixed. Nothing going on around her mattered. It was fascinating, and terrifying at the same time.

After a few minutes, the Old One stopped speaking. He took his hand, and smeared it over Doug's body, until it was covered in blood. He then brushed his hand against the rock, whispering again the foreign words. He then covered his face with his hand. He seemed to be smelling the blood. Finally, the ghoul bent down and bit into Doug's neck. Janine's face flooded with tears as she watched. The Old One was drinking blood from Doug's neck, like she had seen in all the vampire movies she had ever watched. She could hear it. The guzzling sound. The slurping sound. The sound of death. And it had come from Janine's hands. She wept, on and on, until she seemed to be running out of tears. Finally, it was all over, and all she could hear were her own cries, drifting slowly out into the vast darkness.

26

Janine woke in total darkness. She was in what seemed like a cave. She quickly jolted up and looked around her. It was impossible to see a thing. She felt in her pockets. Her phone was there. She got it out and checked it. It was almost 2 am. She heard rustling sounds near her. "Who's there?" she yelled. Janine flashed her light to her right, and saw a dead body. She screamed. Then she heard a voice coming from behind her on her left.

"It's fine. Relax."

It was the Old One. Janine jerked up and shone her light on him. He held his hand out to block Janine from seeing his face. "Turn out the light," he said. Janine did as she was told.

"What happened?"

"You passed out at the rock. I brought you here."

"Where are we?"

"Still in the park. We are in the caves. The Lenape caves. This was my first home."

"Who is that? That's not Doug." Janine pointed to the dead body.

"This is a tracker. He was following you. I saw him near the rock. I waited to see what he would do."

"What did he do?"

"He and a woman were following you. They followed you and your sacrifice to the rock. After the ritual, they tried to attack you. I handled him. The other got away."

"Got away?"

The Old One chuckled. "Well, there's only so much one can do. I could have either chased her around the park or brought you here before anyone suspected you of murder. I chose to protect you."

"Then why didn't you kill him instead of DOUG!"

"The ritual won't work with a tracker."

"What's a tracker? Why is he following me?" Janine became exasperated and raised her voice to the Old One.

"This was a human, but he was turning. He would have become a vampire if I hadn't taken care of him. The woman he was with must have turned by now."

"I don't understand."

"A tracker is a human who has been bitten by a vampire, but not turned yet. Their human instincts, senses, and knowledge must still be used to find someone. This tracker was being used to find you."

"But why?"

"You are a dangerous person, Janine Gomes. You know more than most humans about what we are. Some vampires don't like that."

"Vampires are tracking me?"

The Old One paused. "Yes. You are being targeted. They clearly want to see you neutralized. They are afraid of you."

"BUT WHO ARE THEY?"

"They are the ones you asked me to help find for you. They are the ones responsible for all the crimes you're writing about. They are...well, they were, my friends."

"Other vampires?"

"Yes. Vampires that I created. Vampires that I led. Vampires that Gregory Painter knew, vampires that followed me when I met him."

"But they don't follow you now?"

The Old One stood and walked to the entrance of the cave. He looked to the ground. "Yes. They aren't my friends any more. They broke with me."

"Why did they break with you?"

The Old One turned and walked toward Janine. "That's a story for another time. It has no relevance on what you asked me to do." The Old One sat down on the ground next to her. "Now, we must discuss our game plan, and what we must do to stop them."

Janine gave the vampire a puzzled look. "So, you are going to help me?"

He chuckled again. "Yes, Miss Gomes. You held up your end of the bargain. I did what was necessary to gain my strength. The ritual worked; it was honored by the ancestors. I now have the power I need to do what is necessary."

Janine started to cry again. "By killing Doug."

"I didn't ask you to bring him, or anyone else you knew. I needed a human to complete the ritual. A human with blood coursing through his or her veins, that hasn't been corrupted yet by a vampire's bite. That's why a tracker can't be used. You chose to bring him."

"I....guess I was being naive. I'm sorry I brought him. Even if he was a boring man, he wasn't a bad man."

"Then we must honor his life by using his death to our advantage. We must stop the Nameless."

"The nameless?"

"He is the vampire responsible for the attacks. He was never given a name when I turned him, so we called him the Nameless. I believe he also goes by the name of Man, because...he resembles one."

"How original. He's acting alone?"

"No. He's not alone. There are at least three other vampires with him."

Janine frowned. "Who are they?"

"There is another who follows him. His name is Jairoz. He's a cunning and dangerous creature. He knows our language, our customs, and our history quite well."

"Any others?"

"There's the other tracker he sent for you, the woman. She would have turned by now. And Azul. He's a bit foolish and headstrong. There could be others, but I won't know until we find them."

Janine stood and started pacing around the cave. "Okay, help me here. How can we stop them? What can we do?"

"What do you know about vampires? What films and books have always told you, correct?"

"Yes."

"Well most of that is wrong. And silly, facetious nonsense." The Old One grumbled under his breath. "All this about wooden stakes and garlic and crosses. That's not accurate. It's all fiction. Neither do we all sound like Bela Lugosi. And we aren't all from Transylvania, either."

Janine started laughing. "Okay, then where are you all from?"

"Again, a story for another time. What you really need to know is how to kill one of us. Because if I'm to do this, I will need your help."

Janine sat and listened. The Old One described how the vampires worked, where they lived. How they could be killed. In sunlight, if you exposed their face to the direct sun, it would kill them. Otherwise, a human could only kill one by removing its head. The Old One described Man, Jairoz and Azul to her. The Old One had turned them all. He was the oldest vampire in New York City, but wouldn't reveal how old he was or why he was helping her kill them.

"Let's just call it revenge," he said. He stared at the tracker's body. "Stay away from this one. He's sick. He's got the virus. The humans are getting sick and dying from it, aren't they?"

"Yes." Janine adjusted the mask on her face. It was covered with grass and dirt, remnants of her experience at Inwood Hill Park hours earlier. The Old One laughed at her as she messed with the mask. He walked over to a small chest he had hidden in the cave. He opened it and removed a dark bandana, with designs on it. They looked like stars. It was too dark to make out what they were.

"I made this many years ago," he said, "to help protect my face in the sun. I don't go out anymore in the daylight, so you may wear it. It will help protect you from the demons that haunt your race. This virus."

"Thank you." Janine took the covering from his long, slender fingers. They were claw-like talons stained in blood. Doug's blood. Janine took the bandana and smelled it. It smelled of must and moth balls. She couldn't see it very well in the dark but wrapped it around her face until it was covering her mouth and nose.

184

"Why are the other vampires attacking humans?" Janine asked the Old One.

"I can only speculate. I think I understand. They are facing a shortage."

"What do you mean, a shortage?"

"Humans are sick, Miss Gomes. The disease. They aren't leaving their homes. That means we can't just pick them up on the streets and take them. We can't drink from them. There is a shortage of human blood on the streets."

Janine understood. A light went off in her. "So they have to be aggressive, and attack humans whenever and wherever they can."

The Old One seemed to nod. "Yes. We have to scavenge for food, like any organism. We must eat blood, or we will slowly starve and eventually die."

"Can you drink from humans that have the virus?"

"It would make us sick. It wouldn't kill us. Imagine drinking milk fresh from a cow that hasn't been pasteurized. Your stomach isn't used to it. You would vomit it up. That's what it's like."

Janine tried her best to stare into the Old One's eyes. "Then why aren't you with them? Why aren't you out there attacking humans if there's a shortage?"

The Old One grunted and turned away from her. "You ask far too many questions."

"That will be my last one for today. I need to know. Why aren't you with them?"

He breathed in and out, slowly. He raised his head. She could feel his eyes piercing through her. It was terrifying.

"I eat rats, cats. I even eat humans from time to time. Like today. But I don't indulge. Every vampire I have ever known that ate humans for sport, ended up dying a violent death. Killing for sport is against my code, against my beliefs. It's dishonorable. That's one of the many reasons why I don't hunt with them, Janine Gomes."

Janine had a million more questions, but sat in silence. The Old One, she could tell, was sensing that she was restless and still confused. He chuckled again and walked away from her, deeper into the cave. "Now, sleep Miss Gomes. In the morning, you will wake and go about your life. The other tracker will leave you alone for now. We have scared her. You will hear from me again soon."

The sound of his footsteps slowly disappeared. Janine lay her head back down on the ground, thinking about everything he had said to her. As soon as her eyes closed, she drifted off to sleep.

27

The female tracker had turned by the time she made it back to the museum. She was now a fully-formed vampire. She craved blood. She mauled a human in Inwood Hill Park as she ran to escape the Old One. She drained the human, a homeless man, of its blood. By the time she had reached the museum to return to Man, she was feeling the sickness. She trembled as she presented herself to her new lord.

"My lord, the girl....she lives...she was helped," she said. She started to retch while speaking to Man. Man laughed at her while she puked up blood and intestines on the museum floor. Jairoz turned away at the sight of it.

"She must have drank from a human with the virus," Jairoz said.

"Exactly. That's exactly what she did," Man replied. "She's still too stupid to know any better. And her senses aren't developed. She wanted to just grab the first human that walked by." Man kneeled down and stroked the woman's head with his hand. "Don't worry my sweet, you will feel better in a while. I will teach you how to hunt, as I was taught by my first master." He smiled and continued to stroke her blonde head. "Where is the other tracker?"

"He was captured, by the vampire."

Man stiffened up. His eyes glared at her. "What do you mean, the vampire?"

"There was a vampire at the park, where I followed the girl. She led this man to the park, where the vampire attacked him." Man paced all around her in a circle as she told the story. She continued.

"This man, he was a friend to the girl. The....vampire drank from him, my lord, near a rock."

"WHAT ROCK?" Jairoz loudly jumped into the conversation.

"I don't know. It....it was at Inwood Hill Park."

Jairoz rushed over to Man. "The ritual. My lord, the vampire must have performed the ritual of healing."

Man stared into space, thinking. "Impossible. We are the only vampires left in this city. There is no one else who would even know about the ritual."

"What of the Old One?" Jairoz asked.

"THE OLD ONE IS DEAD."

"Yes, my lord."

"I killed him years ago." Man walked the floor of the museum, kicking the female's vomit off of his shoes. He placed his hand again on the head of the female. He stroked her hair. "This woman, Gomes, is smarter than we accounted for. We have underestimated her. We won't make this mistake again." Man grabbed the female's hair and raised her off the ground. "Find the woman again, my sweet. Gomes. But don't kill her. She will lead us to this....vampire. Report to us every hour until you find her. Then report again when you see her with the...vampire. Then we will dispose of them both. And you will get to feed off of her. You alone."

The woman smiled. She longed to make her first pure kill. "Thank you, my lord." Man released her and she ran from the room. Man watched her go. He stared again into space. He lost himself again in his thoughts. Memories of the Old One and the times they shared together. Hunting in Times Square. Drinking blood from animals, then from humans. Finding places to sleep in the middle of the bustling city, surrounded by danger. Man closed his eyes and smiled. He missed his mentor. He was his friend, his closest friend. His only true contemporary. They would play chess together on Sunday afternoons in Washington Square Park. They would dress as homeless men and play that game of strategy, sometimes for hours. They wouldn't even hunt then. They would sometimes play against humans, and always win. The greatest thing the Old One had taught him was that not every human needed to be a target. You could use them for amusement; to entertain yourself, from time to time. Man took a deep breath, putting aside the memories. He then turned to Jairoz.

"I tell you, friend, that vampire is dead. I cut his throat years ago. When we left him," Man said.

"Yes my lord. But who then is this vampire she speaks of?"

"She doesn't know what she is yet. She just turned. She is most likely mistaken."

"Still, shouldn't we prepare for the possibility?"

"If this thing was truly one of us, we would have sensed it in all these years. It was probably a human who believes he's a vampire. Some type of cannibal that eats human flesh."

Jairoz grimaced. "Humans are truly sick in the head."

Man laughed. "Yes. They are, my friend. Still, Janine Gomes eluded us because of this...person. It attacked her and this other human she was with. So it either knew she was being followed and helped her by scaring off the trackers, or it did us a favor and took care of her. We will find out soon enough."

"And if it's helping her?"

"Then we will have to just finish the job we started. If the virus doesn't get her first. It's spreading like wildfire."

"Yes my lord. I have read the day's newspaper, 700 dead over the last few days."

"Hundreds if not thousands more have this sickness. It will be much harder for us to hunt. We may have to resort to eating animals again."

Jairoz frowned. "I hope it doesn't come to that."

"So do I." Man stared at the pile of intestines and blood that lay all over the floor. It began to smell.

Man covered his face with his arm. "I will clean this up, Jairoz. I want you to follow the female. You may need to help her find Gomes and this...vampire. Observe what she does, how she hunts. Step in and help her only if necessary. She should be able to tell soon which humans have the sickness."

"The female had it when she was human. She still has it inside her. She will probably be sick for a good while."

"That's right. She may not even survive. Who knows? This is all so new and strange. I thought that after more than 100 years of existence I would have seen everything."

Man and Jairoz walked together to the entrance of the museum. The moon shined brightly in the sky, but dawn would soon be coming. The two vampires stared out into the green forest that surrounded the museum; the trees and flowers that shielded it from the outside world. It was a beautiful place. Man watched Jairoz step out into the night, hunting for the female and following her scent. Man spent a few more moments soaking in the beauty of the wilderness. He then turned and slipped back into the vast darkness the museum provided for them.

28

Joe Zarga had already left three voicemails for Janine by the time she reached the office. He was clearly on yet another rampage. Janine went straight to his office as soon as she got into the newsroom. Zarga yelled for her to come in.

"Janine, I'm afraid we have more bad news."

"What is it now?"

"Doug Cross. His body was found in Manhattan this morning. He was killed."

"WHAT?" Janine did her best to win the Academy Award for Best Actress. She was interested to learn what the Old One had done to cover up his crime.

"He was found in the middle of a street, 207 near Broadway. Apparently he was the victim in a robbery. There had been a fight, a struggle, between him and the robber it looks like. He and another man were found shot. The police have someone in custody."

Janine raised her eyebrows. Wow, the Old One had gone to great lengths to cover this up. The other victim was probably the tracker she had seen in the cave. Who though would be in custody? Her mind kept turning and turning.

"Who do they have in custody?"

"Some young punk with a long criminal record for dealing drugs and stolen guns. He was found at the crime scene with two handguns on him."

She cringed at his inappropriate description. Janine was close to breaking down. This person was going to get blamed for the death of Doug and the tracker. That meant they would be facing life in prison.

"You OK?" Zarga's question startled her.

"Yeah, I'm fine. I'm sorry, this is just a lot to take in."

"You're goddamn right it is. That's it. I can't handle this. I've lost two employees in the last few weeks, both murdered. The virus story is just totally out of control. Westchester it seems is no longer a hotspot so I'm bringing Grossman down here to help you and Erica with coverage."

"Got it."

"But everyone, I mean EVERYONE, is going to be working from home the next week. Maybe longer. We've been dancing with the devil here for far too long Janine. You're working from home. I can't afford to lose any more of my employees."

"You think that Doug's death is related to the bite attacks?"

"Don't you?" Zarga glared at her. He adjusted his glasses.

Janine paused. "I...I'm not sure."

"You're lying Janine. I know you are. You know a hell of a lot more than what you're letting on. What aren't you telling me? Who is doing this?"

"Joe, I need some time.."

Zarga raised his hand. "FUCK that. If you know something that will help me protect the people in this newsroom, then you better tell me right now. Or you and I are going to have a long conversation with the police. So please think carefully about how you answer this."

"Send everyone home. Have everyone work from home. They will be safe. It's not safe to go out at night, you're right."

"Why? What's happening?"

Silence. Janine looked down. She held her head in her hands and rocked back and forth. Tears were coming yet again. She looked toward the window. For a moment, she thought she could see Doug standing by it, covered in blood. She let out a sob. Zarga walked around his desk and put his hand on hers. "Janine," he said, "please let me help. Please. You can talk to me."

"I think...that what's happening might be unexplainable by natural means."

"What does that mean?"

"I think that something....evil is happening. By forces that are truly dangerous."

"Gangs? Mob?"

"Something worse Joe. Something that's not....human."

Zarga processed her comment for a moment. Then he turned around and slapped his hand on his desk. "No, Janine, don't go Hammer Horror on me. This is New York City 2020. You're talking about ghosts and zombies and stuff?"

"Vampires."

Zarga laughed nervously. "That's the funniest thing I have ever heard. Janine, I get it. You're exhausted. You're stressed. I'm sorry I make your job even harder. I don't want to believe me, but we are so fucking understaffed it's not funny." He stopped and sighed, sitting back down. "When this virus story gets under control, I want you to take a two week vacation. Go anywhere. Relax and recharge. I just need you to hold on a little while longer. I know you aren't sleeping much and what's happening around us is terrifying enough as it is. You're getting bad and crazy ideas into your head."

Janine sat and soaked in what he was saying. She couldn't believe Zarga was acting like this. He continued speaking after a few moments of silence.

"I'm sorry. I shouldn't have exploded on you just now. I'm...I'm scared too, Janine. My wife is staying inside, she won't even go to the store. My kids, they're away in Europe and having to come home because of this." He looked around his office. "I just...I want this all to end. I want to be able to go to baseball games. Take my wife to the theater. I want us to be able to go back to just covering regular crime and city stories. Not this." More silence. "I swear though, Janine, Doug

195

Cross is the last of my employees I'm going to have to bury."

That hit Janine like a fire truck. She broke down. The tears flowed. Zarga got up again and put his hand on her shoulder.

"It's okay," he said. "Go home. Take the day off Janine. Tomorrow, you start working from home." Zarga reached into his desk and grabbed a box of tissues. He plopped them onto the desk and handed one to Janine. She wiped her eyes and breathed deeply. After a few more deep breaths, she thanked Zarga and walked to his door.

"Oh, one last thing," he said. "Beverly needs you to call her. Something about a source she was running down."

"Thanks Joe."

"Janine, I won't ask again who is behind this, but if you know something that I need to know....tell me right now. Or, soon. Tell me very soon, please. Now go home. Get rest. And let's come back with fire tomorrow."

***

Janine called Beverly on her cell phone as she went back to her desk. She kept a backpack in her bottom desk drawer. She opened the backpack and threw in some things she needed from her desk: her AP stylebook, a dictionary, a small thesaurus and three reporter's notebooks. In them she had all of her notes

196

she had kept about the bite attacks, going way back to before she had ever met Gregory Painter.

Janine threw everything into her bag and turned on her computer. She placed her flash drive into the computer to back up all her stories and file notes she needed to work from home. Beverly's cell went to voicemail after a few rings. Janine started putting all her files on the flash drive, when Beverly called her back.

"Hey Bev."

"Janine, I called up the Pennington today to see what was going on with Gregory Painter. I spoke to that Heidi woman again."

"Okay. Was she as rude to you as she was to me?"

"Yeah. Janine, I just wanted you to know. Gregory Painter passed away last night."

Janine nearly dropped the phone. Her heart sank right back down into her stomach. When would all this pain ever end? She got the phone back up to her ear. "Sorry, did you say he died?"

"Yes. I'm sorry. Heidi found out this morning. The hospital called them. He died from the virus, apparently. They're going to transport him to the morgue."

"Does she know if he had any next of kin?"

"I didn't ask. You want me to?"

"No, it's okay. Do you know when they are supposed to get his body over to the morgue?"

"I think sometime this morning. Or afternoon."

"Thanks Bev. I'm going to head over there. See if I can get a report from the coroner to make sure Heidi was telling you the truth."

"You think it could be something else? Foul play?"

Janine thought about that question for a while. "I don't know. Probably not. He was old and very sick. But....I just need to know for sure."

Beverly coughed on the other end of the line. "You doing okay?" Janine asked.

"Yes. Sorry about that. I'm eating breakfast and trying to speak at the same time."

Janine's stomach cried out for food. She couldn't even remember the last time she ate. She really needed to soak in a hot bath, take a nap, and have a large plate of her mom's scrambled eggs. Janine's mom made the best scrambled eggs in the world. Janine could almost forget about her other problems when she thought about those eggs.

"Janine?" Beverly had asked her a question and she didn't even know it.

"Sorry Bev. Say that again."

"Do you need me to call the Pennington again? Follow up with Heidi about anything?"

"No. Thanks Bev. I will take care of it. Oh, by the way, just so you know I'm working from home the rest of the week. So don't call the newsroom number, just my cell if you need me."

"Okay. And Janine, they apparently are having a hard time getting all the bodies to the morgue. Erica has a story about it in today's paper. Some of the bodies are waiting on ice in trucks to be shipped over there. So you better call them before you head over. Make sure his body isn't waiting at the hospital."

Janine believed it. The last she had heard, nearly 400 people were dying from the virus every day. It was putting terrible strain on the hospitals and funeral homes. Janine thought of the nurse Grace, working long hours and just trying to help. She still felt bad for lying to Grace to get into the hospital.

"Okay, thanks Bev. I will call the morgue first and see if Painter's made it to them yet. Call me on the cell if you need me." Janine hung up. She needed to still get some more files on her flash drive. As she performed the mundane task, she thought of Gregory Painter. He was a good man. He was trying to do the right thing at the end of his life, to help rid the world of an evil that he'd been mixed up with years before. She thought of the last time she'd seen him, in that hospital bed, riddled with pain and sickness. He didn't even know who she was. The poor man deserved a better ending to his life. Janine was determined to help him have it. She was going to tell the story, the true story, about who was responsible for the bite attacks, no matter the cost.

29

Gregory Painter's body lay on an ice slab in a truck
next to the hospital where he died. She'd found that
out after dozens of phone calls and frustrating
conversations. Janine wasn't allowed to see the body,
despite how much she complained to the coroner and
hospital officials. She was only allowed to take a
photo of the truck, if she chose to do so for press
purposes. Janine decided against it. Instead, she said a
prayer. She didn't much believe in the power of
prayer, but she remembered that Gregory Painter did.
Besides, she thought, it couldn't hurt.

Janine walked away from the truck; away from the
hospital. She just walked. Farther and farther away
from it, through the residential neighborhoods of the
Bronx. These were old neighborhoods that had once
been filled with Italian immigrants. Now, it was filled
with Dominican and Puerto Rican residents, and
African American residents. She passed a pastry shop
that she absolutely loved; it was closed. So was the
pasta store that made fantastic linguine noodles.
Everything was closed. These streets, usually so busy
with students and tourists, were empty.

Across the street from the pasta store was a church. It
was a very old Roman Catholic church. Janine hadn't
been inside a church in years. Her father was a lapsed
Catholic, and would go on Christmas to midnight
mass. She'd tag along to make him happy. She liked
the pomp and circumstance; the Christmas hymns that
would fill the halls with merriment. Her favorite
hymn was Oh Holy Night. She stared at the beautiful

structure, with its majestic facade. There was a statue of one of the saints outside, in a little courtyard. In front of the statue were roses, where people came to show tribute. It looked so peaceful. One little element of peace in a world that was tearing itself apart.

Janine walked inside the church. She was surprised the door was open. There were a few people praying. They were spread out so she couldn't see their faces. She wondered who they were, if they had lost someone too in this terrible pandemic. Had they lost their job? Were they regular church goers? Or like her, were they just hoping for a miracle? Janine slipped into a pew and knelt down on the kneeler. She said a prayer for Gregory Painter. And Doug Cross. And Ben Rodriguez. And for family and friends. Finally, she said a prayer for her.

Janine could hear someone enter the church behind her. She was too lost in prayer and thought to bother turning around to see who it was. She continued to pray. She was open to anything if it meant helping clear her mind. She thought about that last Christmas mass with her dad. It was only a few months ago, but it seemed like much longer than that. The person who entered the church had moved into the pew not far from her. Strange, she thought. Then, the person spoke.

"You are far too reckless with your personal safety."

Janine opened her eyes quickly and turned towards the voice. It was the Old One. What was he doing here, she thought. He was covered in clothing, and his face was covered with a mask and hood. If he had been human, he would have been sweating bullets. She knew however, the truth. He was as far from human as you could get.

"What are you doing here?" she asked.

"You're being followed. You knew that already. And yet you wander around alone in a strange neighborhood."

"I thought vampires could die in the sunlight?"

"Only if our faces are exposed. If you cover yourself like this, you can move around."

"Well, fine. I'll be more careful. Now please don't bother me right now. I really don't want to talk to you."

"You saw Painter's body?"

Janine looked at him strangely. "How did you know he had died?"

"I heard you back there. I'm sorry that he passed away."

"What do you care? You used him too, didn't you?"

The Old One snorted. He looked at the stained glass around him, admiring the craftsmanship. "It's been so long since I have been to a place like this. It's really quite stunning."

"What about Gregory Painter?"

"Gregory Painter helped me, yes. He helped us, my kind. He lied to protect my identity, and in return he was given protection for his life. I liked him very much. He was a very intelligent human. We talked about history, and literature, and music. Things that I used to appreciate when I was a human too."

"You aren't human. You probably never were. You used Gregory Painter, you're using me. That old man died alone in a hospital bed, I went and saw him. He gave all of his life to writing and journalism, and died a broken old man. He deserved better."

"I was human too, you know."

"I doubt it. And how the hell did you stage Doug's death to look like a gun crime? The police are putting the blame on an innocent man, you know!"

"I am very old, Miss Gomes. I have been perfecting the craft of hiding my identity for centuries. I was born in Pennsylvania. Bucks County. 1745. It was summer. My mother told me it was the warmest day of the year. I was the oldest son in a family of four. We lived downtown, in a small house. My father was a blacksmith." The Old One looked around the church as he told the story. He held onto the pew in front of him with his claw-like hands.

"How then did you become a vampire?" Janine asked him.

The Old One sighed. "I joined the Continental Army, during the war for Independence."

Janine was stunned. "You were a soldier in the American Revolution?"

"Yes. I was a colonel in the Continental army. My father knew a general that was stationed in Philadelphia, a man by the name of Edwards. John Edwards. He made me a colonel because he and my father fought together in the Seven Years War."

"So what happened?"

"I was given command of 75 men. And 25 natives who were forced to volunteer. We were stationed at Fort Washington. It was here in the city."

"I've heard of it. Somewhere in Washington Heights."

"In the fall of 1776, our orders were to defend the fort at all costs from the British. Under the command of General Washington and a man named Greene. We had to stop the redcoats from going up the river. There were so few of us to defend it; we all knew we were going to die." He paused. He looked to the ceiling and wrapped his hood tighter around his ashen face. "I never wanted to be a soldier, Miss Gomes. I wanted to make my father proud, but I didn't care about patriotism, I didn't care about any of the things we were fighting for. I didn't own land. I hardly paid any taxes. I never had any problem with British soldiers before the war. So I didn't want to die, fighting the war."

"But you did."

The Old One was silent. He sat looking at the altar. He'd hung his head for several minutes before he finally spoke again. "I deserted my men. I deserted the army, while the British were attacking us. I fled. I watched my men be captured and I fled...they begged me to help them." He turned to look into her eyes. She could see the grey darkness where his eye sockets were. She could feel his guilt, his remorse, flowing out of his disfigured body. "I brought this curse on myself, Miss Gomes. I brought shame to my father's name."

"So what happened then, after you deserted?"

His voice trembled as he spoke. "I...knew I couldn't return to Pennsylvania, as a coward. And so I jumped in the river. I drowned myself. And....I became....I became this." He pointed to his body, his clothing, his hood.

"Because you committed suicide, you became a vampire?" Janine was confused. She'd figured he had been bitten in a bloody, messy fight with one.

"There are many ways to become one," he began. "I took my own life in shame, after committing a great sin. That's one of the ways."

"What about the others? Jairoz and Azul and all of them?"

"I turned them. I created them. They were all humans too, at one point in time. They all followed me. When Painter met us, we were living in the tunnels. Then we were ambushed, our home was being taken over."

"By the mole people." Janine was beginning to understand.

"Yes. That's what Painter called them too. But they weren't moles."

"Don't worry. It's just an expression. Go on." Janine smiled.

"These.....moles were moving into our tunnels, and Man and Jairoz were very angry about it. We argued over what to do. My belief was that we could live with them and give up some of our home to them, to share with them. Man and the others disagreed. They wanted to flush them out, or to kill them. So they did, over my objection they started killing them. One night, Man came to me and told me that he and the others were leaving. He challenged me."

"Challenged you?"

"For leadership of our clan. A challenge is given, when a vampire wishes to take over the leadership of his or her horde. It is an old law of our order."

"What happens?" Janine was fascinated. She listened intently.

"It's a fight. Like, a duel, between you humans."

"Those don't really happen anymore."

"I'm aware, Miss Gomes."

"Sorry, please go on. So he challenges you. You had to fight him."

"You fight with your....your hands, I suppose you would understand that, yes. You fight with your claws, your hands. When the first blow is given to the other's throat, the challenge is over." He pointed to his throat, and gestured. "The winner of the challenge is the leader of the clan. The loser is given punishment. It is at the winner's discretion, along with the opinion of the rest of the group."

"So they decide what happens to the loser. And I'm guessing you were the loser?"

The Old One breathed a long sigh. "Yes. That's correct. I was beaten. Man cheated. He used a small weapon to prick my throat. A small knife he'd concealed during the challenge."

"Why didn't you say something about it?"

"I did. Oh, I did. It didn't matter. Regardless of what I said, the rest of the clan wanted Man to be in charge. They wanted to kill the mole people. They wanted me gone. So they sentenced me to die. Man slashed my throat." The Old One removed a part of his hood so Janine could see a small part of what looked like a very large scar.

"It looks grotesque. So they tried to kill you."

"They thought they did Miss Gomes. I played the role to perfection. They thought they had killed me. But they didn't. You remember I told you, how to kill a vampire?"

"Yes........sunlight directly to the face, or.....you remove the head."

"Yes. That's correct. Very good, Miss Gomes. They didn't finish the job. Man thought he did, but he didn't stay to make sure. I survived. Barely, but I survived. I stayed in the tunnel for the last 30 years or so, at 91st street. Surviving on rats, feral cats, and squirrels that the strega brought to me. Doing nothing to attract any attention. I hadn't spoken to any human or other vampire, until you came to see me. I was too weak. If a vampire doesn't taste human flesh, they become very frail. They can survive, barely. But they must have something to feast on. I needed to perform the ritual to regain my strength. Without it I couldn't defeat Man and the others. So I needed you Miss Gomes, and you needed me."

"What's to stop you from killing me when this is over? Why should I trust you?"

"Have I ever lied to you about anything? If I wanted to kill you why didn't I just do it the first time you came to see me in the tunnels?"

Janine pondered that question for a moment. It did make sense. He could have killed her then and he had never shown her any aggression. "I'm not Painter," she said. "I plan on telling the truth. The man blamed for killing Doug is innocent. People have to know what's happened here, what's been happening. The vampires are a danger to society."

"I don't plan on stopping you Miss Gomes. I've never hurt you or any other human without good cause."

"If it stays that way, you won't be included in my stories. Why did Painter decide not to say anything?"

"Why do you think?"

"He blamed the mole people for the bite attacks. So..."

"He protected Man and the others. In exchange for his own life. He knew I couldn't protect him from them, so he made a deal with them. He would keep quiet about them, and in return, they stayed away from him."

"Jesus Christ."

"Not a wise thing to speak the name of Jesus in vain. Especially in a church." The Old One laughed.

"I doubt you're offended."

"Very few things offend me, Miss Gomes. Not after you've lived as long as I have. Not after you've seen as much as I've seen."

"I can imagine. Let's get out of here." Janine started to rise out of the pew, but the Old One quickly put his hand on her to stop her.

"We can't do that just yet, Janine." The Old One smiled at her. Janine shuddered while looking at him. He was up to something.

"Why is that?"

209

"They're here, Miss Gomes. They're watching us right now. I can smell them."

"Who's here?" Janine's eyes widened in fear.

"They're very close. Two of them. The woman. And....it's not Man. Probably Jairoz."

"What do we do?"

"I told you you shouldn't be so reckless with your personal safety. It's too easy for them to track you."

"Ok, but what do we do right now?"

"Oh don't worry Janine, they'll make the first move. In fact, they are about to right now."

30

In the next moment, a figure soared from above them. It was hiding in the choir loft, and knocked Janine down against the pew. It pinned her to the ground, salivating on her face. Janine turned her head to avoid the spit and kneed it in the crotch. The female vampire groaned and lurched backwards. It smelled of rotten vegetables and body odor, causing Janine to gag. The female growled and threw herself back onto Janine. Janine fumbled for the pepper spray she had hidden in her purse, kneeing the vampire as much as she could and as often as she could. It growled and screeched like a cat being strangled. This thing was hideous, Janine thought. It was dripping blood from her mouth. It was covered in scars and what looked like warts. Who the hell was she? She looked like she'd been a beautiful dark-haired, dark skinned woman at one point in time. She was probably in her late 30s, maybe early 40s. She had tattoos covering her arms, one Janine could tell was of someone who had died. There were birth and death dates inked on her bicep, around a rose. It was probably very pretty before she became this ghoulish soldier in the army of the undead.

The woman scratched at Janine's throat and eyes. Janine tried to shield herself as best she could with her elbows, but it wasn't working. The Old One was somewhere away from her, but she could hear him struggling with something. It must have been another vampire. She yelled for him to help, but he was off in another part of the church, far away from her. She didn't even know if he could hear her yelling.

Janine tried to grab a hymn book on the floor next to her. She slipped her fingers around it, but wasn't able to get a hold of it. She moved her body a bit to the left, and tried again. It worked. She was able to clutch it and with all her might swung the book around her body till it smacked against the vampire's head. The female's head then swerved to Janine's right where it hit hard against the wooden pew in front of it. The vampire crumbled to the floor; stunned. Janine wriggled away from it and got her hands into her purse, pulling out her pepper spray. She quickly crouched into a defensive position, backing away from the vampire, and out of the pew. She reached the aisle and straightened her body. The vampire got on its knees, even angrier than before. She let out a loud moan and screamed. She searched the pew and church, until her fiery eyes found Janine. It terrified Janine to her very bones. This bitch was pissed.

"Stay away!" Janine roared. "HELP ME! HELP!" She screamed it as loud as she could. The sound of her booming voice thundered against the walls of the church. It filled the room. She tried to look in all directions, to find the Old One. He was in the back, next to the church entrance, yelling in some language Janine didn't understand. It must be the language of vampires, Janine thought. The woman's head turned toward the sound of the Old One. Janine quickly seized her chance and started running in the other direction. It was a mistake. The female vampire,

Janine didn't realize, could fly. She quickly leapt into the air onto Janine's back. Janine hit the marble floor of the church hard, knocking her out of breath.

The female was again on top of her. It rustled her and kicked her, it thrashed against Janine with great force. Janine was out of energy. Out of adrenaline. Out of ideas, on how to stop it. It was about to rip into Janine's flesh with her fang like teeth. This is the end, Janine thought. She had no gas left in her tank. She was exhausted. Emotionally and mentally. Just play dead, Janine thought. Play like you're dead. So she did. Surprisingly, the vampire started to slow down. Janine's hands clenched as she tried as hard as she could to remain still. Her right hand tightened around the can of pepper spray. Janine couldn't tell if the can was right side up or down. She had to take the chance. So she did. She hit the spray button, taking a leap of faith.

***

The Old One could feel the force of Jairoz slam into him, but it didn't affect him as much as he thought it would. He could feel the strength of a hundred vampires flowing through his body. The ritual had truly worked. Jairoz's ambush barely made him flinch. He grabbed Jairoz by the head and flung him toward the altar in the front of the church. Out of the corner of his eye, the Old One could see the female launch toward Janine. His first instinct was to help her, but the female still didn't know how to control her body, her muscles, her joints, as a vampire. Janine was putting up a hell of a fight. The Old One smiled as he walked toward the front of the church, closing in on his enemy.

"It's impossible," Jairoz said as the Old One moved towards him. "You---you were killed. How did this happen? We....retired you."

"I'll show you, my old friend," the Old One replied. "I have waited a very long time to show you the extent of my abilities."

He leapt onto Jairoz. The two wrestled on the church altar, ripping at each other's hoods and clothing. Part of the Old One's clothing ripped, exposing his leg. The sunlight burned a small hole in his flesh. The Old One quickly covered up the mark with his tunic, while his hands forcefully rocked back and forth, digging into Jairoz's body. The Old One ripped Jairoz's flesh with his long claws. Jairoz was strong, but couldn't move fast enough to continue defending himself. He thrust his head back against the altar and then swiftly swung it forward, head butting the Old One. The move allowed him to squeeze free of the altar.

The Old One spun around and fell off the altar. He hit the ground, but quickly raised himself back to his feet. Jairoz was running toward the only other parishioner in the church, an older woman dressed in black. The woman moved slowly and was trying to escape. The Old One could see his opponent's plan. Jairoz was going to turn her, to help them in their efforts to kill him. He could cut him off, if he acted quickly. Then, he heard Janine screaming. He turned to look in her direction. She was on the ground, the female on top of her. Janine was flailing her arms and spraying pepper spray onto the female's face. She was running out of energy, he could tell. The Old One quickly soared into the air and crashed into them.

The female vampire screamed as she was thrown off of Janine. The Old One quickly shoved her into the church's remembrance candles that flickered brightly. The female caught fire, in a matter of seconds. Her decaying flesh was ablaze and illuminated the church in a bright orange light. Janine stared in horror as the Old One shouted at her. She couldn't tell what he was saying at first. Then, it all came to her.

"KILL HER!" The Old One pointed to the elderly parishioner. "Kill her, now!"

Janine froze. She stood like a statue watching the madness unfold around her. The female vampire was crashing into the church walls, burning and screaming. The Old One was in hand to hand combat with Jairoz, throwing punches and kicking. The elderly woman was on the church floor, bleeding from her neck. Jairoz had clearly bitten her.

"KILL HER JANINE! SHE WILL TURN SOON! SHE WILL KILL YOU! STOP HER NOW WHILE YOU STILL CAN!"

Janine couldn't move. She heard the Old One's screaming, but she didn't heed it. She gagged. Her stomach was hurting her. She trembled, and fell to the ground. She held on to a pew to steady herself. She was going to vomit. She tried her best to hold it in. She exerted herself as hard as she could. She closed her eyes. Doug was there. She could see his face, his smile. She could hold on no longer. She began vomiting. She spit on the floor, on the pew, on the hymn books. She couldn't see what was happening around her. If she were to live another moment, it would be because of the Old One. She was ready to surrender. She was too tired to fight any longer. Her mind, her body, her very soul, were broken.

***

The Old One locked his claws into Jairoz's shoulders. The fight had carried on for longer than the Old One had anticipated. Jairoz was wearing down, but his spirit was still strong. Jairoz was a noble opponent, a true warrior. A proud member of the vampire race. He was the Old One's favorite, all those years ago. The Old One remembered, then and there, how they had met. Jairoz was a soldier too, but in the American Civil War. He was wounded at Gettysburg and had returned home to New York City, to heal. He became an alcoholic, wandering the streets, tormented by the visions of his fellow soldiers beaten and bloodied at Antietam, Fredericksburg, and finally Gettysburg. The Old One found him passed out drunk, in the streets of what was now Greenwich Village. He turned him then and there, and nursed him. He taught him how to hunt, how to fight, and most importantly, how to behave as a vampire. With dignity. With grace. Not to be a common criminal, or an oversexed cretin. When the Old One was challenged, it hurt him more than anything, that Jairoz had decided to stand against him. His closest friend.

Jairoz kicked at the Old One again. He kicked with his feet, his legs. For Jairoz, every part of his body could be a weapon. The Old One liked that too, about him. He didn't need a fancy weapon to make a kill. He just needed his intellect. The Old One took the blows, knowing that with each thrust, Jairoz would lose a little bit more energy. All the Old One had to do was wait it out, and stay alert. Finally, he saw an opening. With a kick, Jairoz had exposed the left side of his neck. With one fluid motion, the elderly vampire swung out his claw forcefully toward Jairoz's neck. It landed. The Old One's claws sliced into his throat, squirting out blood that soon became flowing out like a small water fountain.

Jairoz dropped to the ground. He had enough energy for one last attack, the Old One could tell. There was still a flicker burning in his eyes.

"We...retired you," Jairoz said. "I saw you die." He then lashed out with his claws. The Old One parried, shoving his opponent's hands to the ground. The sound of bones crunching. The sounds of moaning, of pain being released from a vampire's body. The Old One kicked Jairoz in the head. The motion threw him toward the ground. His head smacking against the marble floor.

"KILL HER, JANINE!" the Old One screamed. He could see the elderly parishioner crawling on the floor, about ten feet away. She was moaning silently the orders that Jairoz had given her. She would be turned soon. Her blood was creating a river along the marble floor, flowing toward the altar and baptismal font.

"Your guardian is weak," Jairoz whispered. He started laughing, coughing up blood.

"She's not my guardian."

The Old One kept screaming at Janine. She wasn't moving. She wasn't doing anything. The Old One sighed in frustration. He kicked Jairoz again. This time on the other side of his neck. Blood spurt out again violently. He was nearly finished. The old vampire was about to shout again, but then he saw her start vomiting on the floor.

"She....has the virus," Jairoz whispered.

The Old One stared at her, watching her. Then he glanced at his prey. His old friend. In that moment, he remembered the very first kill they made together, on a dark city street near City Hall. There was a magician, with a traveling show. He set up a tent there in downtown Manhattan, to entice the businessmen on Wall Street to pay a few pennies for entertainment. They tracked him for days, to study his habits. Finally, one night following a performance, the Old One and Jairoz followed the magician home. They nabbed him, and his assistant. They feasted on both. The Old One remembered the taste. The flesh. The blood. The hair. The sweat. The joy of being able to teach a young vampire the way of their existence.

The Old One held out his right claw away from his body. He knelt down, picking Jairoz up with his other claw. He held his face very close to his body. He looked into the eyes of his fondest companion. He smelled his blood. He could smell the elderly parishioner, the two trackers, and at least three other humans Jairoz must have drank from in the last week.

"I gave you this life," the Old One said. "It's only right that I should be the one to release you from it."

Jairoz breathed heavily. He was very weak. His strength was quickly draining from him. He formed a small smile, with his bloodied mouth. His fangs were covered in his own blood. He stared into the eyes of the Old One for a moment longer. Then he closed them.

The Old One thrust his right claw into the center of Jairoz's throat. He pushed it in farther and farther, until he had nearly removed Jairoz's head. He then with great speed pulled his arm back. Blood again spurted as Jairoz's head dislodged and fell to the floor. It rolled a few feet away from him, until it finally came to a stop in the center aisle of the church.

***

Janine had completely shut down. She clung on to the pew with both of her hands. She leaned against it, breathing heavily. She could hear it all around her. The sounds of hell. The female vampire was still trying to put out the fire that was raging all over her. She was rolling all over the church floor. She could

219

hear the Old One killing the other one. The female parishioner was talking to herself. She didn't want to look at her. All Janine knew was that she was going to continue clinging to that spot.

She could hear the Old One walking near her. He was saying something in another language. He picked up something. With all her might, Janine managed to open her eyes. The Old One was standing over her with a hymn book in his hand.

"Breathe, Janine. Just breathe."

He walked over to the elderly parishioner. He said something to her in that foreign language. Janine deduced it must be a special language between the vampires. The old woman didn't say anything. The Old One lifted the hymn book over his head, as if to strike the old woman. Janine closed her eyes again. The sound of the hymn book crashing down. The sound of the old woman's head being bashed in. The sound of her screams. In a few moments, it was over.

The Old One stood over the body of the old woman. Janine watched him closely. She no longer trusted him. He was an animal; a hurricane of violence and anguish, destroying everything in his way. Janine watched him breathe in and out, heavily. He stared at the cross that hung over the altar. He stared at the stained glass windows. Finally, he walked to the female vampire, who was rolling on the floor trying to put out the flames. He patted her all over, and spoke to her in the vampire language. The female finally calmed down and stopped shouting.

Janine could barely breathe. The horror of the last several minutes was finally ending, and her emotions were slowly coming back to her control. She leaned over the floor, away from her vomit. The smell was stinging her nostrils terribly. The vomit, the blood, the guts of the bodies all around her. She couldn't look at them. She was making noise again. She realized she was hyperventilating. The Old One came over to her. He put his hand on her shoulder.

"Breathe slowly Janine. Deep breaths. Open your mouth. Now breathe."

He stayed there for what seemed like an eternity. She finally got her breathing on track again, despite him standing there.

"Can...can you please just get away from me?" she said.

The Old One obliged her. He walked back to the female and sat her up. He spoke to her again, in the language Janine couldn't understand.

"What are you saying?" Janine asked.

"She's going to lead us to Man. She's going to help us end this."

"Why....why did you kill the old woman? Why did you want me to kill her?"

The Old One was using something to tie the hands of the female vampire. Janine couldn't tell what it was. "She was turning," he said. "Jairoz bit her and was going to use her against us." He turned to face Janine. "You couldn't have saved her. It was too late. If she hadn't died, she would have killed you. And we need you to stay alive."

Janine lowered her head and stared at her own vomit. She took a few seconds before she spoke again. "I'm not a murderer. I'm not like you."

"You have to do what is necessary, Janine Gomes, if you want to defeat evil. You already know that. When you brought me Doug, you made a specific choice. You chose to do what was necessary."

Janine burst into tears. She kept picturing Doug's face in her mind. "Fuck you asshole!" She yelled across the church. The Old One was silent, finishing up the job on the female. Again, he spoke to the female in vampire speak. He yelled back to Janine.

"Are you willing to kill Janine, in order to stop Man?"

"I won't kill a human."

"That woman was no longer human! And neither is this woman, Janine Gomes. Any vampire can turn a human through a single bite. At that point, they are cursed. They must be killed or they will turn into a foot soldier in the army of the undead. Like me. Are you prepared to kill in order to stop that from happening?"

"Fuck you."

"Cursing me won't stop anything. It won't keep Man from destroying your city. It won't keep this one from killing more humans for food, either."

Janine didn't answer him.

"I need you to understand what has to be done, Janine. I need a willing partner. I need someone who will kill if that's what it takes."

"I've come too far to turn back. I can't let Doug Cross die for nothing. I can't let Mr. Painter die for nothing. Or Ben." Janine wiped her tears with her sleeve.

"Then you do understand."

Janine examined her conscience. "Yes."

"Good. Now rest. Sleep. I'm going to bring you home. Then I will make her take me to Man. I will end this."

Janine was about to argue with him, to demand that she be with him for the confrontation. She was too exhausted to speak. As soon as she got her next word out, she fainted from the fatigue that had taken over her body.

31

When Janine woke, she was in her bed. She quickly
threw off her covers and looked for her phone. It
wasn't on the nightstand, where she would usually
find it. She rubbed the sleep from her eyes and got up
to look at her alarm clock. It was 3 in the morning.
She must have slept for at least 12 hours, possibly
longer. She was angry at herself for not being able to
stay awake and go with the Old One. She was also
frustrated at losing her temper at the church. She was
clearly stressed out from everything.

Suddenly, she heard a noise coming from her living
room. Janine quietly got up and walked to her
window, where she kept a baseball bat that had
belonged to her grandfather. He taught her the best
ways to swing it with force if you ever met an
intruder. She wielded the bat and crept to the
doorway, very carefully. She pressed her head against
the wall. She tried to make out what the sound was.
After a few moments, she realized a man was
speaking. The voice was very quiet, but then suddenly
it got much louder:

"If we shadows have offended, Think but this, and all
is mended," the voice said. "That you have but
slumbered here; while these visions did appear. And
this weak and idle theme, no more yielding but a
dream."

Janine couldn't make out who it was. She slowly
lifted the baseball bat, raising it next to her head. She
then quickly rushed out into the living room

brandishing it. The Old One stood in the center of the room, reading from a book. Janine screamed and quickly dropped the bat.

"A Midsummer Night's Dream, Miss Gomes," he said. "The words of William Shakespeare. The character Puck, to be precise. Act Five, I believe."

"YOU SCARED ME TO DEATH!"

He raised his hand and put the book down on Janine's coffee table. He then placed his hand on his chest. "I'm sorry. I was just reading some of my favorite monologues aloud. This one is one of my favorites. A very nice book! I found it on your shelves."

"Yes, I know the play. I played one of the lovers in my high school's production."

The Old One smiled. "How fascinating. I prefer the tragedies myself. You know the Scottish play? Tomorrow, and tomorrow..."

"YES." Janine interrupted him. "I'm familiar with it."

"A masterpiece. One of many that he wrote."

Janine grew impatient."What's going on? Did you find Man?"

The Old One picked up the book again and carefully placed it back on the shelf where he'd found it. "Yes, I know where he is."

"Good! Let's go!"

"Sit Janine. Rest a little while longer."

"I don't want to rest! Where's the female vampire? Is she going to lead us to him?"

The Old One sat in a rocking chair Janine had in the apartment. He rocked slowly back and forth while answering her pesky questions. "I took care of her. She won't be bothering you anymore."

Janine paused. She imagined what fate the female vampire met with. "So where is Man?"

"Janine, I need to tell you something."

"What?"

"It's not going to be easy to hear."

"Just say it."

"You have the virus."

Janine felt her blood chill. Her face scrunched up. "You're saying this to keep me here."

"No. I would never lie to you about something like that."

"Why are you saying this, then?"

"Vampires can tell if someone has it. We can smell it in human blood. Jairoz knew it, back at the church. I didn't, because I haven't been around enough humans lately to get the sense of it. But I do know now."

"I don't have the virus."

"Why did you vomit then, back at the church? Why are you running a fever now?"

"I'm not running a fever now."

"Check your temperature. You're over 100 degrees."

Janine glared at him. It scared her, how much he seemed to know about her. She was frightened. She walked to the bathroom. She pulled out the thermometer from her medicine cabinet. The Old One followed her, keeping his distance. He stood in the hallway, leaning against the wall.

"I think you're wrong," Janine said.

"Possibly. But you forget, I'm more than 200 years old. I've had a great deal of experience when it comes to these things."

Janine scowled at him and put the thermometer under her tongue. She waited, her heart beating rapidly. She could hear the clock ticking on the wall of her living room. The Old One stood there silently, watching her. She could feel his eyes looking into her very soul. It made her uncomfortable. Sensing it, the Old One turned and walked back into the living room. He sat in the rocking chair.

Finally, the beeping sound. Her temperature had been checked. Janine stared into the screen, transfixed when she saw the numbers. 100.2. He'd been right. Goddamnit, she thought, was he wrong ever about anything? She tossed the thermometer into the bathroom sink. He yelled at her from the other room.

"Well?"

"It's......100.2. You're right."

"Do you believe me now?"

Janine's mind raced. She thought about everything she knew about the virus. It was bad news to have a fever, but that didn't mean it was the worst case scenario.

"It could be a cold. A stomach bug. Food poisoning."

"I guess I haven't done enough to earn your trust. I only defended you. Killed three vampires. Brought you here safely for you to rest."

"I'm sorry, OK! I'm sorry. I....I'm just scared." How could she have gotten the virus? Then she remembered. The hospital. Gregory Painter. She'd exposed herself to it.

"That's understandable. I'm sure everything will be fine. I can smell it on you, but it's not terribly strong."

Janine decided to change the subject. "So where's Man?"

"Somewhere in the city. I won't tell you where."

"Why?" Janine asked angrily.

"Because you're in no condition to go there. I know you more than you think I do. I know if I tell you, you'll go, when you should be resting."

"Some of my friends are dead because of him. I've come too far to turn back. I told you that before."

"I admire your courage Janine Gomes. It isn't a normal human that would have the guts to come and find me in that subway tunnel. I knew from the first time I met you, you would take this to the end. But you're sick. The virus is inside you. You need to take it easy, or you could make it worse on yourself. Or someone else."

"So what are you going to do?"

"I'm going to kill him."

"Not without me, you're not."

The Old One smiled. "Very well. You're aware that you're risking your life by going after him, even if we do defeat him?"

"Yes."

"You realize that if we don't defeat him, it means your death?"

"Yes."

"You realize-"

"Cut the bullshit. Do I know what the stakes are? You know I do. I just told you. I've lost friends. I've risked my life. I'm sick. I might die. It doesn't matter. This fucker needs to be stopped, that's all that matters. And the people need to know who he is and that we were the ones who stopped him."

Janine's eyes flickered with the fire of anger. The Old One nodded his head. "Very well, Miss Gomes. Tonight, our battle plan begins."

32

Janine sat and typed out a story on her computer, about everything that had happened so far. She felt that if she were to remember everything, she would need an outline first. She wrote down dates, times, places. She tried to describe in great detail what the vampires looked like, and what Gregory Painter had told her. Joe Zarga had left lots of messages for her while she'd been sleeping. She e-mailed him back since it was the middle of the night, letting him know she'd tested positive for the virus, and needed to quarantine at home. She told him she'd been sleeping most of the day and apologized for the tardiness of her message. She was sure he'd be blowing his top through his computer again once he'd read it, but at least that should keep him off her back until this was finished.

The Old One paced around her apartment. Janine kept glancing at him out of the corner of her eye, wondering why he couldn't keep still. He clearly was excited about what was to come.

"So tell me about Man," Janine finally said. "What's his story?"

The Old One stared at her. He finally stopped pacing after a few moments. "I turned him. Many years ago. Gregory Painter knew him. Man wanted to kill him."

"I think he mentioned that to me."

"I turned Man sometime around the time the stock market crashed."

"29"?

"Yes, I believe that's right. It was after the first war in Europe, I remember that. He was a soldier too. All of us were. There were seven of us. Now, there are only two."

"Two?"

"Myself and Man. We're the only ones left."

"What about the others then?"

"Azul, something must have happened to him. He died. We turned him after the Second World War. There were twin brothers, who served in Korea. Saava and Naif. One of them challenged me and failed. The other asked to be freed from the curse. I killed him."

"He just asked and that was it?"

"He was going insane. He would have tried to kill us. He couldn't handle the way we lived, the way we had to survive. After his brother's death, he broke down and begged to be released. I honored his wish."

"And then Jairoz, whom you killed in the church?"

"Yes. He was my closest friend of the group. I mourn him."

"That's six. You, Jairoz, Man, Azul, Saava, Naif."

"Hmmmm..."

"But you said seven."

"The last one is the strega."

"That's the witch, who brought Gregory Painter to you?"

"Yes. She's not a vampire. She helped us, she lived with us. She fed us. She nursed us to health. She wasn't one of our kind, though. She left after I lost control to Man. She was forced out. I saw her last nearly 30 years ago, I don't know where she is now. Possibly, well...probably dead."

"Are there other vampires?"

"There are many around the world. Most are in Europe, places where our kind was born. There are several in the United States, too. I'm the oldest one in New York, but there are a few even older than I am in the West. The first ones that ever came to America, hundreds of years ago on ships."

"What's the name of the oldest one here in the states?"

"His name is too long to mention. He came here as a slave from Africa in the early 1600s. He dwells in San Francisco now, I believe. I learned about him from my mentor, and taught my kind about him."

Janine kept writing. The Old One didn't seem to mind. He told her more, about his mentor, who had left New York for Europe more than a century before. He told her about why he was able to go inside a church, when his ancestors could not.

"Vampires evolve, like humans do, Miss Gomes. The first vampires could not get into holy ground. As more and more humans became vampires, the vampire took on more of their former human characteristics. Humans who were holy men and women could walk onto holy ground when they turned. Then, more and more vampires were able to do it. Now, almost any vampire can. That's why holy water doesn't work on us anymore, either, or garlic, or so many of the other things we discussed."

Janine was fascinated. The Old One told her about the vampire language, but refused to teach her how to say any of the words. To do that, would be like inviting a curse on herself, the Old One said. He told her how and why some humans became vampires after death, and others did not. A person could become a vampire by being bit by one, or by committing suicide after having murdered a person, and not asked for forgiveness first. It was how he had become one. Once a vampire had been born, there was no way to turn back into a human. Death was the only release, and not by suicide. A vampire could be retired by being murdered, if the head were to be removed. The only other option was sunlight, directly into the vampire's face.

"Painter mentioned something to me about a guardian. What's that?" Janine asked.

"A guardian is a human who makes a blood pledge to a vampire. The human is given immunity from being turned, and protection. In return, the human pledges to serve the vampire for the rest of their natural life."

"That doesn't sound that bad."

"At the end of the human's life, the human must make a final sacrifice to the vampire. To complete the partnership. The human may give their life, or the life of a loved one, in return for everything they have received."

"I see." Janine definitely didn't plan on becoming a guardian. "Was Painter your guardian?"

"No. He wanted to be, but it never came to that. Man got in the way." Janine frowned. She wished she'd had a chance to talk to Painter more about it.

Janine took notes on everything and organized it into a word document. She started writing the story on her laptop. How the attacks started again, 30 some years after they stopped. How the vampires had lived in New York, and how Man had taken control of them. She wrote and wrote until she fell asleep sitting over her computer.

33

Two weeks passed. Janine worked from home, speaking with Zarga every morning. She still attended news meetings via computer. The virus kept spreading, and deaths were nearing 500 every day in the city. The virus cases accelerated, too. Then things just got worse. Protests started, anger at keeping businesses closed. Janine could hear yelling at night, the protestors only a few hundred steps away. She didn't go out at all. She'd order in food and groceries, and the Old One would visit her every few days.

One morning, her phone rang. It was Zarga.

"How's it going?" he asked.

"I'm still sick, but feeling better. I don't have a fever any more, but I get chills. How are things there?"

"My wife's mother got the virus. She's in a nursing home. Some of the residents got it. She's on a ventilator at the hospital."

"Oh no! Joe, I'm sorry. That's terrible."

"Thanks. We are going to get through this. I don't know if she can make it, but we are hoping and praying for the best. I'm glad you're feeling better."

"Thanks Joe. I have some more copy ready for you. A thousand words on the bite attacks series."

"Ok send it over. Will take a look. How's it going with the protests? Grossman's been covering it pretty well for us."

"Yes, I've got copy on it for you too."

"Ok. Ok, when can you have it for me?"

"This afternoon. I just need to get confirmation from the NYPD on some background information. I think I need to talk to another source too. I've interviewed a couple of small business owners that had their stores looted."

"Sounds good Janine. I'm telling you, that bite series might get us some national recognition. You're the only reporter in the city that stayed on it. It would be fantastic for us and the readership circulation to see you nominated for a Pulitzer."

"A Pulitzer?! Jesus Joe, that's kind of you but I don't know if it's that good."

"Don't sell yourself short. You've been doing a great job with it. Whoever your source is, it's been a godsend for us."

Janine chuckled to herself. A godsend? It was a deceased disgraced former journalist and then a vampire that had been her sources. Zarga didn't know that. She wondered if he'd still feel this way if he did know. Janine also hadn't mentioned yet in her series that vampires were behind it all. She'd kept her cards close to her chest. When Man was defeated, then it would be time to put everything out on the table.

"Ok Janine. Keep at it. Send that copy to me today by 3 if you can. I'll edit it for you. We'll get it in tomorrow's edition with Grossman's stuff."

Since Janine had been sick, Zarga hadn't yelled at her once. He'd been surprisingly calm and collected. It was a much smoother working relationship, probably for both of them. Janine wondered how much longer it would last. She hung up the phone and got back to writing. She organized her stories, fact checked them and edited for spelling. Before she knew it, it was after 12 and time to grab lunch.

She made herself a turkey sandwich with stuff she found in the fridge. Janine held on to the refrigerator door, staring inside. She hadn't heard from the Old One, and it was worrying her. It had been three days since he'd visited. Had he killed Man? Had he been ambushed and killed? If she didn't hear from him, how long could she wait before she went ahead with publishing her final stories? She was working herself into a sweat over the stress. She sat down at the dining table to relax. She had to take it easy. The virus was still in her, lurking. She could feel it; it was like toxin inside her body. It was lingering there under the surface, waiting to attack.

The phone rang. It was probably Zarga again. She was sure he wanted to squabble about story length, or some other minor detail he forgot before.

"Yes, Joe?"

"How are you feeling?"

Janine's mouth dropped. The Old One. He'd never called before. In fact, she was shocked he could even use a telephone.

238

"How did you get my number? Where are you calling from?"

"A payphone. I'm not as stupid as you think Janine." He laughed. "Now, how are you feeling?"

"Better. Not a hundred percent yet."

"Good. Because it's time. I will be there to get you this afternoon. Be ready."

The line went dead. Just like that, he was back. No details, just a direct order. She immediately got hot under the collar. He didn't even give her a time! She quickly sat back down and finished her lunch. The stories would have to go to Zarga quicker than she'd anticipated. Be ready, he said. Be ready for what? She had no idea what to expect. She thought about it as she ate the rest of her lunch. As soon as she'd finished, she got to writing again. She had no idea when she'd be needed, and she wanted to be prepared. She finished writing her stories for Zarga by 1 and sent them off to him in an email. She texted him to follow up.

Janine then made her way to her bedroom. What would she need for this showdown with Man? She thought about what the Old One had told her, about how vampires worked. She decided to bring her pepper spray, but also the sharpest and longest knives she had in her knife block. There were two that were very long and very sharp. She rarely used them, as she didn't cook that often. And when she did, it was normally just to make pasta or a salad. She admired

Julia Child, but she wasn't going to try deboning a chicken. She wrapped up the knives as carefully as she could in towels and put them in an old backpack she kept in the back of her closet. It was her college backpack, and she hadn't touched it for several years. She unzipped the pack and carefully placed the towels inside. She hoped she wouldn't cut herself if she needed to reach these in a hurry.

Janine then thought about light. Sunlight to the face could kill a vampire, but she couldn't replicate that. However, she did have a pretty strong flashlight her dad had given her to keep in her car, when she was driving. He said you never knew when you might get stranded on the side of the road at night. She was glad he'd thought of that. The flashlight's brightness might be able to slow Man down if she came face to face with him. Hopefully, it would give her enough time to attack him with one of the knives. She replaced the light's batteries. She then put the flashlight in the pack's front pouch.

Next, she thought of clothing. She shouldn't wear anything too bright. She also shouldn't wear anything too uncomfortable. She chose a black hoodie that she used for running sometimes. She thought it wasn't too hot out, so jeans should work too. She changed as her cell phone rang. It was either Zarga or the Old One, she guessed. She decided to let it go to voicemail. She didn't want to be distracted at such an important moment.

After she'd changed and packed, Janine went back into the living room to check her phone. Zarga had called. He'd left another long voicemail. He was probably complaining about something she'd written. She opened her laptop and called him back. He answered on the second ring.

"Janine, your story about the looted businesses needs some more work. We need to get comment from the NYPD."

"I haven't heard from them, Joe. I've left two messages with my contact there."

"Well you've got two hours. What's the rush to send me the story if it's a few hours before the deadline and you don't have all that you need?"

"I might have to run out and meet a source for the bite series."

"Run out? Janine, you're sick! You need to stay home."

"Just to a coffee shop a few blocks away."

"Coffee shop? Everything's closed."

"Sorry, not in the shop. Outside the shop. It's a place where we meet."

"Janine. Stay home. Can't you just talk to them over the phone?"

"It's important, Joe."

"What's more important than getting better goddamn it!" He was back to his old self, short-tempered and stubborn. "Stay home Janine. Talk to your source through another method until you're better!"

"Joe, I'm doing this whether you like it or not. It's very, very important."

He seemed to be very interested and pulled his anger back slowly. "What do you mean?"

"I'm so close to cracking this whole thing open. I'm just so close to meeting the mastermind of these attacks. The man behind it all." Her pun wasn't intended.

"Janine, is there any other way you can do that? I really don't like the idea of you going out of the house."

"I feel much better. I've quarantined for two damn weeks. I'm doing this."

Silence on the other end. She wasn't sure what Zarga was thinking. She tapped her finger on her laptop, then her desk, while she waited for his response. "Joe?"

"Janine, please stay home. Please get better. I don't want to have to go to another funeral this entire fucking year. If you're really this close to something big, you could be in danger. Now please, do I need to call the police, to have them check up on you?"

Janine was enraged. "No Joe, you don't need to call the cops. Because you don't have any responsibility at all over what happens to me. I quit." Janine hung up and threw her phone across the room. She grabbed her backpack, threw on a light coat, and went out of the house.

As soon as she started walking down the stairs, she could feel it. Her chest tightened. She started coughing. The virus was still in her lungs; in her chest. It tightened its grip on her as soon as she tried to physically exert herself. She coughed until it was a strong hacking sound. She perhaps wasn't ready for what was about to happen next. She stood on the staircase, leaning back against a pillar. Breathe, Janine. She kept telling herself. She breathed in slowly, then out. In slowly, then out again. She did this for five minutes. Finally, she felt ready to start walking again. She was able to get down the rest of the stairs without too much trouble.

It was still light outside. It had rained not long before she came out. She could see the puddles clogging up the drains on the street. The sidewalk was covered with little puddles of raindrops. She usually loved the smell of the city right after it rained. It was unlike anything she'd ever seen out in the desert. She hated getting caught in the rain without an umbrella, which seemed to happen more often than she'd liked. Still, she usually enjoyed the rain. Not today, though. She couldn't smell that well, and what she could smell was not very appealing. She could smell what seemed like rotten pork; barbecued food that had been smoked too long. It was disgusting.

Janine started walking down the street. She slowly wrapped her backpack over her shoulders, until it settled on her back. She didn't know where she was going. She just had to get out of the apartment for a while. She wondered if the Old One was keeping an eye on her and watching the building. If that were the case, he was probably following her now. She walked in the direction of Washington Square Park. It was only a six minute walk away from her apartment. She could sit in the park and try to refocus her breathing. She could just take in the trees and the benches, the squirrels and the chess players, if there were any out and about. That would be lovely, she thought. A small reminder of what could be again.

Janine turned the corner onto Walker Street. She was near the park now. She could almost see its famous arch. Then she saw it, rising from the misty New York sky. The arch of Washington Square Park. She would be there soon. She smiled.

Then the world went completely to black.

34

Janine woke up in darkness. It wasn't the park, nor was it her apartment. She couldn't see anything. She moved to get up, but she couldn't. She was too weak. Then she realized, as she moved her limbs, that it wasn't weakness. She was tied down. She jerked her wrists, and realized they were tied. She was tied with rope, to a pillar or something like it. She practiced her breathing exercises as she slowly tried to loosen her wrists. She struggled with them for several minutes, to no avail. She was tied up, and wouldn't be moving anytime soon.

She decided to sit on the floor. She leaned back against the pillar. She tried to look around, but it was just too dark. She felt around the floor with her legs and feet, to see if she could find her backpack. There was just emptiness, all around her. She tried to feel around with her elbows, her arms, her neck and head. Nothing. She was helpless.

Then she heard it. A rumbling sound coming nearby. It sounded like a subway train! She must be near a station. She started yelling. Her voice was still weak from the virus, but she could get a few good, strong notes out. It wasn't going to work, when the train was coming. The rumbling and screeching of the train's brakes drowned out all sound. She scrunched her face as her ears were bombarded by the sound of subway brakes. She could also smell the effluvium of subway brakes hitting the track, it was like the smell of burning rubber. At least her sense of smell was coming back. She couldn't smell badly smoked barbecue anymore.

Then there was light. The subway train was lighting up the area around her! She quickly got a look around. It was a subway platform. She was on a subway platform, but there was no one there. It didn't make any sense. She could hear the train, and see the reflection of the train's lights though. The train was moving, but it was around the corner from the platform where she was sitting. She couldn't see the train, and the conductor wouldn't be able to see her. There was an opening about ten feet away, that must have led down to another platform adjacent to the train. The lights were bright and illuminated the small platform where she was sitting. There were what looked like ceramic tiles on the walls, in green and beige. A green door was boarded up on the other side of the platform, across from where she was tied. There were no other people there, though. Janine's mind raced. She broke into a sweat again. Where could she be? Then she guessed it--it must be another abandoned subway station.

As the train passed, Janine struggled back up to her feet. She exerted herself so much, her voice gave out on her again. She cursed herself. Her voice wasn't strong enough to alert anyone on the train that she was there. She would have to break free from the ropes and get down to the other platform, so they could see her. It was her only shot. The train finally completed its pass, and the platform was quiet again. Then she could hear it.

Footsteps. One long, sliding footstep. Then one short. It sounded like someone was walking with a limp. Was it the Old One? Why would he bring her here? He must have had to leave his spot at 91st street, she guessed. Go to another station. There were so many questions racing through her mind, when she finally heard the voice.

"Janine Gomes. Born on September 20, 1992. Daughter of Peter and Laura Gomes of the state of California. The youngest of two children."

Janine didn't recognize the voice. Still, it knew who she was. It knew of her family, her birthday, who her parents were. She sat back on the ground as a horrific chill went down her spine. She knew exactly who this was. There was only one person who it could be. The other vampire. Man.

"Reporter for the New York Daily Reporter newspaper, a daily in New York City. Covering public affairs, crime and courts, and general assignments."

The figure was on the lower platform, where the train had just passed. She wondered if he was a passenger on the train, or if he'd been there on the platform the entire time. She'd find out soon. Man was moving toward her, inching closer with every step.

"Wh....what do you want?" Janine sputtered.

"You stick your nose into too many things Miss Gomes. You've made my existence much more difficult."

247

"I know who you are. Man. What do you want?"

"Who has been helping you?"

"You know who."

Man paused. "I want to hear it from you. Who is it?"

"The Old One."

She then saw him. The outline of him. It could barely be seen in the darkness. He turned the corner, and stood in the opening. He then slowly pushed himself up the steps to face her on the platform.

"You lie," he hissed.

She could hear another train coming down the track. It slowly began to illuminate the platform again. As it powered itself into the station, closer and closer, she could see more and more of him. The light from the train gave Man a backlight as he towered over her. She nearly shrieked when she saw him. He was horribly disfigured. A large scar covered his face. He had only one eye, the other eye socket was barren. There were large crevices that looked like deep valleys on his cheeks. His caramel skin appeared blood red, like sand from the desert. He was grotesque.

"He's coming here, to stop you."

Man limped his way right in front of Janine. She could feel his rotten breath on her neck. She avoided staring into his eye.

"You're lucky, Janine Gomes. I would turn you right now if I could. But you stink of sickness. The virus is feasting itself inside of you. It's coursing through your veins, even now."

"He's going to kill you."

Man turned and started walking away. "The Old One is dead, Janine Gomes. The strega must have been telling you lies. The same as she did to Gregory Painter. I killed him more than 30 years ago."

"Jairoz thought that too."

Man quickly spun around. "WHAT?"

"Jairoz thought that too. Right before the Old One ripped his head clean off."

Man rushed back to her and struck her hard across the face. His limp was a charade. He didn't have a problem moving. Janine felt blood spurt out of her mouth. One of his claws had dug itself into her face. The force of it forced Janine back to the ground. She breathed heavily, hatred growing in her eyes.

"Enough of these games Janine Gomes. I won't turn you but I can still kill you, slowly, painfully, and to my great pleasure." Man roared. "Now, if you value your life, you will cooperate with me. Who is helping you? Where is he? Tell me, or feel everlasting agony."

He hit her again on the other side of her face. Her head whipped around in the opposite direction. He grunted with pleasure as Janine moaned with pain once again. She slowly staggered back up to her feet when another train started rolling into the station. Janine looked around as the light illuminated the platform once again. Man turned to look as the train's brakes once again made its horrific shrieking sound.

"The 6 train. Turning itself around in the crown jewel, Miss Gomes. This was the original City Hall station. Opened in 1904, on the IRT line. You would have loved it in its day, I'm sure. Tilework, skylights and chandeliers. Men in suits going to work, and women in beautiful gowns going to the opera, hustling and bustling all over this platform. I feasted here quite well, Miss Gomes. It's....like a home to me."

Man slowly caressed the walls with his claws. He kept talking as Janine started to exert herself, trying to get out of her constraints. She tried feeling in her pockets for anything she could use to cut the rope. She couldn't reach them. She kept straining, but Man had bound her hands very well. The train was leaving the platform below, and the lights began to fade. Just before it was completely dark again, Janine saw it. Her backpack. It was sitting on the other side of the platform, close to the green door that was boarded up. She had to find a way to get it, or have him bring it to her. Her mind started working again, coming up with ideas.

Man turned to face her again. "Now the train only turns around here."

"Sounds wonderful," Janine said.

Man laughed heartily. He began moving toward her again. "You're quite humorous. Much more so than Ben Rodriguez."

The anger returned. Janine's face was flushed, as red as a strawberry. "You killed him, didn't you?"

"He chose not to cooperate. I gave him a choice Miss Gomes. The same I'll give you. A chance to save yourself."

"Like the one you got Gregory Painter to accept?"

Man laughed again. "Painter? My goodness, that was a long time ago. How's that tedious old fool doing?"

"He's dead. The virus killed him." Janine stared into Man's eye with as much hatred as she ever had for anyone.

"Was he the one who helped you?"

"I already answered that question." Janine snarled at him.

"Now, now Miss Gomes. I know you think you hate me now, but I am only being fair and honest. I don't kill anyone unless I absolutely have to. Ben Rodriguez chose not to help me. He insulted me when I gave him an opportunity to live. So yes, I killed him. I gave Gregory Painter a chance to help us as well, and he listened. He did exactly what we asked of him."

"He died a lonely, broken man! You broke his spirit."

251

"I did nothing to that man. I spared his life!"

Janine glared at him. She was filled with rage. Her eyes lowered to the ground, when the idea came to her. She started breathing heavily. She had one chance to try and make this work. She decided to throw caution to the wind and go with it.

"What do you want from me?" She screamed at him.

Man answered her calmly and directly. "Who helped you at the park? Who killed my tracker? And at the church? Where is he now?"

Janine forced every word out of her with as much anguish, pain and emotion she could pull together.

"I TOLD YOU! THE OLD ONE! PAINTER SENT ME TO HIM AND I HELPED HIM! I GAVE HIM A SACRIFICE. I...." She slowed down. "I helped him kill a man. So the Old One could complete this stupid fucking ritual!"

Man stared at her in bewilderment. Janine breathed, heavily. She then started to hyperventilate. She started coughing. The virus was helping her play the part. "My...my...." she whispered into the air.

"What...what is it?"

"I need...my.."

"WHAT?"

"Asthma....my bag. I need my..."

"Your inhaler."

Janine nodded. She kept coughing, kept hacking. Her mother had asthma, and she would remember as a little girl when her Mom would have an attack during the summer while working in the garden. Janine never imagined then she'd be imitating one of her mother's asthma attacks. She did as best as she could.

Man brought the backpack to her. He did keep his distance though, more than she wanted. About six feet. He was about to unzip the bag pocket which held the knives. Janine violently pointed her leg toward the other pocket. It worked. He moved his claws to the smaller pocket that held the pepper spray. He cut into it with his claws. Janine tried to pull herself away from her constraints as best as she could, exerting her muscles. Her strategy was that the rope would rip and she could get a hand free to quickly grab the pack. Her hands and wrists hurt like hell as she pulled. It wasn't going to work. She'd break her arms if she kept trying.

Man was examining the items in the smaller pocket. It had her pepper spray, an old reporter's notebook from her first year out of college, and some pens.

"There's nothing here to help you," he said.

Janine started gasping. She got down on the ground, and curled up as best she could into the fetal position. Her eyes fluttered. She didn't have to act as hard now. The virus and her exertion were wearing her out and making her nauseous. She got down and hoped Man would give up on the bag. He paused searching. She could feel his eyes on her, watching her closely for movement. Janine kept as still as she could. He crawled closer to her.

"Are you alright? Speak."

Janine kept silent. She moaned slightly. She didn't want to play dead entirely, that wouldn't work. She had to appear very sick and in need of care. Janine knew Man probably wouldn't kill her if she still had information he needed. By now, he probably believed the truth, that the Old One was still alive. But he still needed her help to find out where he was. Who he was with. How much he knew about Man's whereabouts.

"Speak, can you speak?"

Janine moaned again. Man began to get irritated. His questions grew terse. His demeanor was curt. His voice rose in anger.

"Where is your inhaler? It's not here."

Janine didn't say a word. She waited silently in a pile on the platform floor.

"Where is the Old One? If he lives, then where is he? Why isn't he here trying to save you, if you're such good friends with him?"

Janine wondered about that too. Where was he exactly? He had said that he was getting her that afternoon. He never did. She was sure he knew where she was, where Man was. Maybe he was on his way. If she could keep him talking, she could buy time.

Then she remembered she'd left her phone at her apartment. No human knew where she was. If they tracked her phone, it would be there, not here. Her only hope for outside help was the Old One. But now she had to stay on track. Man believed she was sick and in need of help. She had to play it out, to get him to come closer.

"My........" Janine whispered to him, hoping to draw him in close.

"What?"

"Mmmmmm..."

He slid over closer. He was now five feet away. Janine stared at him, hoping to use what basically was a Jedi mind trick. Get over here, she thought. She sent her plea to the heavens, to the spaghetti monster, to the force, to anywhere or anyone who was listening. She had to get him over to her. Four feet away. Then three. Janine closed her eyes tightly. Two. This was it.

"Speak, Janine Gomes. I know you can."

Janine opened her eyes. With as much force as she could muster, she plowed her face right into Man. It hit him in the nose and cheek, knocking him backward in wonder and surprise. Janine quickly took advantage. As he slid backward on the floor, she used her legs to wrap around her bag and kick it back toward her. She lowered her head, but realized it was bleeding from the trauma of the blow to Man. No, her nose was bleeding, spraying out onto the ground. Man would no doubt be longing to drink it. She had only seconds to complete what she wanted. She lowered her bleeding face into the small pocket to find what she was looking for. The flashlight. She found it. She grabbed it with her teeth and whipped her head around. Man was about to take another run at her; she could hear him. Quickly she turned her head to the left and pushed the flashlight to her shoulder. She kept jerking her head onto her shoulder, trying to get the flashlight to turn on. She had to try three times, but she got it. It turned on and blasted its glow in Man's direction. He staggered back, shoving his claws out to block the light from hitting his face.

"Clever creature," he hissed. "But your efforts are futile."

Janine scrunched her head towards her shoulder, to keep the light on him. She couldn't do this forever, she knew. Her head was hurting, her nose was bleeding, and she was in unspeakable pain in her arms and wrists. Still, the light was keeping Man at bay. She longed for the Old One to show up, to clean up this mess and just kill Man. She quickly got that thought out of her head. She had the upper hand, at least for now. She had to find a way to get her hands free, so she could reach the knives in her pack.

"I need to be untied," she said.

Man laughed. "And why would I do that?"

"Because I have information that you want. I know where you can find the Old One."

Man's tone immediately changed. He sounded very intrigued. "Why should I trust you, Janine Gomes?"

"Because I can help you stop him."

More laughter. "You fascinate me, Janine Gomes. What did Kipling say? Oh yes. The female of the species is more deadly than the male. Or something like that. I must say, I'm starting to believe him. I have never met a human female like you. Your will to survive, your will to live, is most impressive."

Janine thought about his response, but pressed on. She literally was up against a wall. "What's your answer?"

Man paused. He took a deep breath, and walked to the back wall next to the boarded up green door. "Name your terms."

"Untie me, and release me. Allow me to write what I choose in my news series, without any repercussions. I will say you and the Old One orchestrated the attacks, with the other vampires. I'll write that you were both killed. Except..."

"He will be dead and I won't."

"Correct."

"And in return, you will help me find the Old One, and kill him?"

"And allow you to escape, go wherever you want. Everyone will think you're dead. I believe it to be a fair exchange."

"Why should I believe that you even want to kill him, after what he's done for you?"

"He....killed my friend."

"At the rock, in Inwood Hill Park?"

Janine lowered her head. She wriggled with the flashlight, using her shoulders and knees to get it to the ground. She kept it pointed in Man's direction, guiding it with her thighs and knees. She felt a little more comfortable, but knew the light wouldn't hold out forever.

"Yes. A sacrifice, at the rock."

"Then I can't kill him, Janine Gomes. He is far too strong to be killed by one vampire. Only you can do it. He trusts you. My only hope is to escape, or reach a truce with him. It concerns me that there's far too much gasoline on the fire to do that."

Janine paused and looked at him.

"Your terms, and proposal, are rejected," he said. Janine's plan didn't work. He wasn't going to release her. The light would go out in a few hours, and he could then rip her body apart.

"I'm more useful to you alive. Like you said, he trusts me. I can still trick him into coming here," she said.

"He's already on his way."

"What?"

"I've known him far longer than you, human. I thought he was dead. He hid himself from us so well. But I am afraid you're right. He's alive, and he's coming here. And when he arrives, I'll find a way to make a deal with him. I'll use you if it comes to that. You're the only loose end, Janine Gomes. We'll have to eliminate you in order to go back into hiding."

Janine glared at him coldly as he continued.

"You know too much. I don't trust you, and when this is over, do you think he will? He's dealt with more humans than almost any vampire ever created. When you aren't of any more use to him, he'll dispose of you. The same way he disposed of all of the humans who helped him over the years. You're not special, nor different. He will kill you. It's his nature."

"You're lying."

Man laughed again. "You'll see, Miss Gomes. You will see." He took in a deep breath and stuck his nose in the air. "The virus hangs on you. You stink."

"Thanks asshole."

"What do you know about it?"

"About what?"

"The virus. What's happening to the city?"

"There are thousands of people who have it. I can't remember the specific number. It's been awhile since the last time I checked."

259

Man grunted.

"I think...well, I know for sure that hundreds have died."

"Where did it come from?"

"Somewhere in Asia, then Europe."

"But what first carried it?"

Janine had to think for a moment. "Bats."

"Exactly. Bats. You disturb the habitat of a bat and it will lash out at you. You disturb the home of any type of animal, and it will lash out at you. For centuries, you humans never learned. You fight each other for power, for greed, for land. Your ancestors stole Manhattan from the natives, right there at the rock, all those years ago. It never satisfied your kind. Now you build your shopping malls and tanning salons and football stadiums, and you wipe out whatever is in your way. And it will finally become the death of you."

"You've killed how many people? But you're an expert on morality, I see."

"I kill to eat, Janine Gomes. I kill so I can survive. And yes, I occasionally kill to keep humans in their place. To remind them that they aren't truly at the top of the animal kingdom. That was a lesson I had to teach the mole people. And they learned it very well."

"He's going to kill you. Whatever hope you have to make a deal with him, it won't work."

260

Man laughed at her again as another train made its way through the station. "Enjoy your comfort while it lasts. That light will go out in about three hours, I would say. And then I will get the opportunity to break both of your arms. Your feet. Your legs. I'll spend this time thinking about which body part I'd like to start with first."

Janine could feel every hair on her body stand up. She broke out in a deep sweat. She hoped the Old One wouldn't need that much more time to find her.

35

An hour or so passed in silence. Janine had to use the bathroom, but couldn't bring herself to do it right there. She fought exhaustion and fatigue. She wanted more than anything to take a nap, but knew the light needed to be guarded at all costs. She kept her eyes on the outline of Man, sitting against the green door. She could feel him smiling and laughing at her. It was a chess game, and Janine was slowly losing.

She constantly fiddled with the constraints, trying to release herself. After about 45 minutes, she was beginning to make a little headway. She could feel the rope loosening around her, just a little. She took breaks every five minutes, to try and keep her circulation going. Her arms and wrists were very sore and tired. She couldn't remember the last time she had to do this much physical work. She cursed herself for not keeping in better physical shape. If she ever got out of here, she'd work out at the gym every day.

Countless numbers of trains kept rolling through the station, assaulting her ears. The sound of the brakes in this enclosed space was excruciating. Man didn't flinch. She wondered how good his hearing was. She'd say something to him when the train was coming through, but he didn't seem to hear her. She'd use those moments to do her most physical work on the ropes, letting the subway trains cover the loud sounds she was making. Still, it wouldn't work. She was pushing a large boulder up a hill. The rope would slowly loosen its grip, then without explanation attach itself tightly to her wrists again. She knew she had to come up with something; she only had a few hours left before the light would burn out.

"How are the Yankees this year?"

Janine was startled. Man had said something, again. He had been quiet for a very long time.

"What?"

"The Yankees," he said. "How are the Yankees, the baseball team, doing this year?"

"I don't think the season's started yet. They were very good last year. Almost made the World Series."

Man sighed. "I loved going to their games. I saw Joe Di play, Mantle, Berra, the Babe. We would go, the Old One, and Jairoz and I. We'd stand in the back of the stadium, waiting for people to come by. We'd sometimes poach, sometimes we would just stand there and enjoy the game. It broke our hearts when the Dodgers left Brooklyn."

"The Old One never spoke of it."

"We were there the day Jackie Robinson first played. I'll never forget it. The people were crowded into the stadium, thousands of them. Most of them were drunk. It was the easiest hunting we ever did. We took seven that day at the park. The most we ever took at a game. The record."

"You're sick."

Man laughed. "It's the nature of what I am, Miss Gomes. You eat, too. You eat animals, don't you? What makes you different from me? Nothing, really. You haven't had to feast on human blood. If you didn't have the virus, I would make you feast on it. Maybe someday you'll have to."

"I'll kill myself before I let you or anyone else turn me."

"Perhaps. But your desire to live is as strong as any human I've seen."

"You're not even really alive."

"Oh, you're wrong, Miss Gomes. I'm more alive than you can possibly imagine." Man got on his feet. "Perhaps you'll let me show you."

"Stay away."

Man started moving toward her, very slowly. "I'll show you, Janine." He had his arms crossed over his face, to protect him from the light.

"STAY THE FUCK AWAY FROM ME!"

Janine pulled against her ropes with all the strength she had. She could feel her wrists, throbbing from the pain, pressing against the constraints. She could slowly feel the rope loosening. Man was only ten feet away, if that. The light was helping to slow him down, but Janine wasn't sure it would work much longer. She could hear another train coming into the station. This was her last chance to set herself free.

Suddenly, she could feel something touch her hands. Someone or something was behind her. Janine tried to jerk her head to see, but as soon as she moved her neck it throbbed in intense pain. It was as stiff as a board. Janine moaned and pushed her body downward. She closed her eyes and carefully focused on what was happening. She soon realized something was gnawing at the rope. Someone was trying to free her! The Old One must have arrived. Janine gasped in both pain and joy. She opened her eyes and looked ahead.

Man was still inching forward, his hands in front of his face. He couldn't see what was going on behind her, and the sound of the train was hiding the noise that was being made. Janine tried her best to breathe in and out, to contain her emotion and excitement. Then, she could feel it. Her right wrist was free. She moved it slowly, to try and free her left one. She couldn't move it well. It may have been broken, she wasn't sure. She very slowly moved her left wrist. It was in better shape. She was able to wriggle it, and shake it until it got away from the rope. Man continued creeping forward. The train was making its way out of the station. For a few more moments, Janine would have the element of surprise. She couldn't afford to waste any time.

Janine crawled over to her backpack. She reached for the back pocket with her left hand. She was able to move it much better than her right. She quickly looked up. Man was only about five feet away. She unzipped the pocket and searched inside for the towel.

265

It was there, thankfully. She carefully pushed the towel aside and felt for the handle of her largest kitchen knife. She found it and wrapped her hand around it. The train had finished its journey through the station. Silence returned.

"Let's see if you can feel this," she said.

Then with all her strength she thrust the knife into Man's foot. He screamed in agony. She quickly removed the knife and slashed into his leg. Then his other leg. Man fell onto Janine. The two wrestled on the ground for control over the knife. Man cursed her in the vampire language, but Janine refused to lose focus. She slashed at him with all her might, like a bird attacking its prey. Cuts on his face, claws, legs, feet. His purple blood, like elderberry wine, flowed all over the platform floor. Janine shouted, cursed, let all the emotions she'd felt for the past several months gush out of her.

In a few minutes, the fight was over. Janine had cut him in so many places, it was impossible to count. He was coughing up his purple blood. He lay on the platform, breathing laboriously. Janine sat back against the platform wall, holding the knife in a defensive stance. She couldn't see who or what had helped free her. The sound of laughter echoed through the subway station. Janine looked around, and then realized it was coming from Man.

"You are the most fascinating human," he finally said. He barely managed to get the words out, due to choking and coughing up blood.

Janine walked slowly over to him. She kept her eyes on him as she reached into her backpack. She found the other knife. She dropped the bloodied one, replacing it with the shiny fresh blade.

"He....will...kill you Janine Gomes."

"Even now, you have to lie?"

"He's...been...duh....deceiving you."

Janine's face wrinkled up. Was this another trick? It didn't seem to be. Man was having trouble breathing and even moving. Still, he was a vampire who had killed several people, including one of her friends. She moved closer to him. Her face over him. The rotting breath filled her nostrils.

"He......lies."

Those would be Man's last words.

36

Janine had fallen asleep on the subway platform. When she woke, she was surrounded by a pool of purple blood. Her bleeding had stopped. She could barely move her right wrist, it was sprained, separated or broken. She sat there, looking at the mess that was in front of her. The vampire's head had been removed. She wanted to throw it down on the subway platform like a football, but she was too tired to do it. She got a better idea. She got up slowly, and picked up the head. She took the towel out of her bag, and cleaned the head as best as she could. Stains of purple blood everywhere on it. She did her best with it, and placed the head in her backpack.

Janine let the rest of the body lay there. She cleaned her knives with the towel. It was now as purple and messy as grapes used for winemaking. She placed the knives in the towel and wrapped everything up. She stood there on the platform, wondering what to do next. She could hear a train making its way into the station. She moved out of the way, so no one on it could see her. She wondered what the passengers or conductor must think, if they saw a decapitated body on the subway platform. As the train made its journey past her, she slowly poked her head out to watch it. There was no one on it. She then remembered what Man had said. This station was used as a turnaround, so there would normally be no passengers on board. She chuckled at the thought of what they were missing. A decapitated vampire laying only a few feet from them.

After the train passed, Janine slowly walked down to the lower platform. As she reached it, she was taken aback by the beauty. Man was absolutely right. This was once a jewel. She stared at the skylight, and the chandeliers that lit the station. It was all breathtaking. She stared down the tunnel where the train had come from, when she saw what looked like a figure on the tracks. Janine was startled. She wanted to yell, but her voice was too tired.

The figure moved closer to her. It walked up to the platform and looked up with large, Sinatra blue eyes. It was an older woman, maybe about five feet tall. She looked like the actress who played Sophia on The Golden Girls. Janine was trying to remember that woman's name, but couldn't. The woman then spoke to Janine. It was a foreign language, but not of the vampires. Janine was about to answer when someone spoke loudly behind her.

"She wants to know if you'll help her onto the platform."

Janine quickly turned around. It was the Old One! He stood on the platform, above her, just a few feet from Man's gruesome body.

"Where the fuck were you!" Janine screamed.

"I'm sorry Janine. But I see you didn't end up needing my help."

"The hell with you!"

"Will you help her?"

269

Janine looked puzzled. Then she remembered the old woman. She turned around and gave her her good arm, lifting her onto the platform. The woman spoke again, and Janine recognized it as Italian. She looked to the Old One for help with translating.

"She thanked you, and hopes you're feeling alright."

"Who is she?" Janine asked while looking the woman over, head to toe.

"This is an old friend. I believe you've heard of her. This is the strega."

Janine's eyes widened. This was Painter's source, the woman who brought him to the vampires all those years ago. Janine thought she must be about 100 years old.

"Does she speak English?" Janine asked.

"No. Just Italian and the ancient language."

"OK. Then.....how old is this woman?"

The Old One roared with laughter. The strega laughed, too, not knowing what was being said. Janine felt bad at saying it, but she was truly in awe of the woman's strength.

"A witch is able to live much longer than a normal human. She's far more powerful than you can imagine," the Old One said.

"Very well. What's she doing here?"

"She's the one who freed you of your restraints, Miss Gomes."

Janine spun around to look at the woman again. She owed this woman her life.

"Please tell her thank you," Janine said.

The Old One did as requested. "What is her name?" Janine asked.

"Bessie is the name she goes by the most."

Janine introduced herself to Bessie. Bessie smiled. She spoke more Italian.

"She wants to know how you feel."

Janine gave the signal of so-so, shaking her hands. Bessie nodded. Janine's eyes flickered with anger again as she turned to the Old One. "Where the hell were you?? I would have been killed, if not for her!"

"I didn't know where you were, Janine. I'm sorry. I had the strega follow you, when I couldn't be around. She was keeping an eye out on your building. She saw Man take you and bring you here. She then told me and I had her help you in any way until I could get here. It looks like I came too late to settle things with him." He nodded to the body. "How did you do it?"

"I cut his head off."

The Old One laughed. "I can see that. You did that quite well. By the way, where is his head?"

"I threw it onto the subway tracks." Janine wasn't sure why she lied, but it felt like the right thing to do at that moment.

He stared into her eyes deeply. She could tell he knew in some way she was lying. He dropped it, though. "Very well. I'm sorry, once again, that I wasn't able to do more to help. But I'm very grateful you took care of him."

"I was able to keep a light on him until I could find a way to stab him."

"Very good." The Old One walked up to the bloodied vampire's remains. He kneeled down and examined them. "We will dispose of the body."

"I'm writing the truth about what happened here."

Janine's words pierced through the subway walls. The Old One and the strega exchanged glances. The Old One stood up and walked down the platform steps to her. He and Janine locked eyes. There was silence for what seemed like a very long time.

"You won't do that."

"Why the hell not?"

The Old One quickly shot back. "Because if you do, you will be implicating yourself in the murder of Doug Cross, your friend."

Janine froze. She hadn't thought of that. It was true. She had helped kill Doug. She brought him to the park, and she held onto him so he couldn't escape.

The memories flooded back into her mind. She could see Doug screaming and trying to get away from her and the Old One. She clenched her fists.

"There's an innocent man in jail. He's going to be charged with Doug's murder, and the murder of the tracker. You committed those crimes, not him. And I.....in a small way, I helped you. I won't let anyone else suffer for the things that we've done."

"So you're prepared to turn yourself over to the police? They'll charge you with first degree murder."

"If necessary......yes. I am going to write about it all, everything. At least that man will have his name cleared."

More silence. The Old One and the strega spoke again. He walked over to Janine, and stared at her for a few minutes.

"Very well. I'm not going to stop you Janine."

"Man told me as he was dying that you are lying to me. I believe him. There's something you're lying to me about. I don't know what it is. Frankly, I don't care. You saved my life in the church and I'm very grateful. I killed Man. I brought you your sacrifice. I figure now that we are even."

"I understand."

"I'm telling the truth about everything that's happened. I'm not leaving out a word. I'm exposing you, Man, Jairoz, Painter. All of it. The public is owed the truth. It should have been told years ago. Painter knew he made a mistake, now I'm going to help him correct it." Janine reached into her backpack. She wrapped her fingers around the knives. She might have to use them again.

The Old One smiled. "I understand, Janine. You will do what you have to do. We will do what we have to do. I'm assuming you have his head, and are going to use it to prove your story. We won't stand in the way."

"Then what are you going to do?"

"We will have to find a new place to live."

"Where will you go?"

"I would rather not answer that question."

"I see." Janine realized that whatever trust there was between them was now gone. She knew he had lied to her, and was keeping information from her now. She was prepared to attack him then and there if necessary.

"How do you say thank you in Italian? I want to thank the strega personally."

"Grazie di tutto."

Janine repeated the words to the strega. She bowed her head and spoke in Italian back to her.

"She says she wishes you luck and good fortune. She put a spell of blessing on you. For good fortune."

Janine thanked her again. She turned to face the Old One. "I guess this is goodbye," Janine said. "I can honestly say I hope we never have to meet again. But I try to mean that in the best way."

The Old One nodded his head. "Janine Gomes, I must say I share the sentiment. Because if we do meet again, I fear that it will be as enemies. Write what you have to about us. The public will decide whether or not to believe it. Some will, and some will not. Those who do believe will come after us, with their cameras. Some will come with their knives and guns."

"Are you afraid of it?"

"I accept it. The world will always be fascinated with my kind. We will always be pursued, and feared. That is the nature of this life." He smiled. "And now Janine Gomes, we must say, adieu forever."

He lifted his hand and bowed. He spoke to the strega and the two jumped down onto the subway tracks. Janine watched as they crossed them, moving farther away from the station platform. She didn't take her eyes off them, as they drifted into the darkness. Another subway train rolled into the station, blocking them from view. When the train passed by, they were gone. Vanished into the night.

37

Joe Zarga slumped at his desk. His whiskey bottle was out; his glass was empty. It looked to her like each word of the story was piercing him like a knife. He kept on reading however. Janine stared at him from her chair. She had written a 5,000 word story about the attacks. All true. She used all of the notes she'd accumulated from her personal experiences and notes from interviews with Painter. She'd even quoted the Old One. There were gaps. She didn't know what had happened to some of the other vampires the Old One had told her about. She didn't know what the Old One had lied to her about. She didn't know how many more vampires were in the city. She knew of at least one, and she knew that was probably one too many.

Zarga refilled his glass. Janine looked out the window. She didn't want to see any more of his facial expressions. She was sure he was deeply troubled by what she had written. She hoped he would publish it, but she couldn't be sure. Zarga sighed deeply. Janine turned back to face him. He was nearing the end of the piece, she could tell.

Finally, Zarga put down the last page she'd written. He looked down at his desk, then over to her. Back to the story, then back to her. He sighed again; a mournful, long sigh. He took another drink from the whiskey. He took his glasses off. After a few minutes, he finally spoke.

"I....I just find this all very hard to believe."

"I have evidence."

Zarga's head darted up. "What evidence?"

"Let's just say I can prove they exist. The vampires. I have something that a scientist would be very excited to see."

"And you're not going to tell me what it is?"

"Well, I don't work for you anymore. Whoever publishes this story will get to see it. If you publish, I will show it to you."

Zarga threw down his glass. "Oh Janine, come on. I understand you were upset and wanted to quit, but you and I both know that you don't really want to resign. You love it here, despite how badly I treat you."

She could tell his last statement was made in jest. She smiled at him. She really did like Joe Zarga, despite his short temper and micromanaging. "My offer stands," Janine replied. "I want double the stringer's fee for this story, and your guarantee it goes to the front page, above the fold in tomorrow's paper. I will show you the evidence once we have an agreement to put the story in print."

"Janine, are you really quitting?"

"Yes. I told you on the phone. I stand by what I said. I'm a freelancer now, and I've got the best damned story in New York City. I'm the only reporter with this information. I'm coming to you first because of our relationship. I respect you very much. I hope you print it. It could definitely help circulation. Possibly get you a raise, or grant money so you can hire some new people."

"Janine..."

"But if you don't agree to print it, there are three other papers in the city that probably will. My next call is to the Times."

"I get it, Janine, I get it," Zarga interjected. "I appreciate you coming to us first with this. I want you to stay, Janine. Take a week off, and go anywhere. Then, when you're back we'll find a way to give you a raise. I'll do my best to give you what salary you want."

"Joe, I'm telling you, I'm a freelancer now."

"A freelancer? Janine, you've READ this story, correct? You're implicating yourself in the death of Doug Cross! Do you really think you'll still get to be a writer if this goes to press? You'll be facing first degree murder charges!"

"I'll do what I can to help the police find him." Janine stared at the floor. "I thought it was all some sort of test. I didn't realize he was actually going to kill him."

Zarga took a deep breath. He looked at Janine with wonder. "You...you're serious, aren't you? You really want us to print this story."

"Of course!"

Zarga ran his hands through his hair. He cleaned his glasses with a cloth and put them back on. "Well...here's something that should make you feel a little better. The guy who was in custody for those murders has been released."

Janine's eyes widened. "Really? What happened?"

"His alibi checked out. He was at a house party and five witnesses can verify he was there that entire night. The guns he had on him were also a different caliber from the one used on Cross and the other victim. So he's out, and charges aren't going to be filed against him."

"Not even for carrying the guns?"

"He's got permits. It was all above board. So he's out, and I wouldn't be surprised if he files a lawsuit against the NYPD."

"Dear God."

"So.....no one is going to go to prison for Doug's murder. You're in the clear, Janine. Unless this story goes to press."

Janine got the hint. Zarga was offering her a way out. She could keep her name clear of danger, if she wanted. All she had to do was ask him to forget what he had just read in the story, about the sacrifice at Inwood Hill Park. It was very tempting.

"Joe. This story is going to go to print. Either at this newspaper, or another one. It's going in word for word, just how I wrote it. And as for me, I'm out."

Zarga looked at her with disappointment. "OK. I'm sorry if you feel I have treated you wrong. I know I should have done a lot better."

Janine put her hand down on the desk gently. "Joe, this has nothing to do with you. I want to take a few steps back, is all. I want to have more control over what I cover, what I write about. I also need to get out of the city for a while. Once the legal stuff is over, of course. Spend time with family. Connect again to the world I keep writing about. It's passing me by so quickly, I barely have time to notice it."

Zarga's frown turned into a smile. "I understand that Janine." He sat back in his chair and ran his hands through his hair again. "OK. Once you get this situation handled with the police, take what time you need. Freelance if that's what you want. When or if you want to write full-time again, give me a call. If you decide not to, then go with God. But who do I get to replace you? We've now got protests erupting all over the city. It's the next big story. I need someone to cover it, today."

"Bev's ready."

"Beverly?"

"Yes. She helped me tremendously on this story, tracking down sources and information. She's doing a lot to help with the virus coverage too."

280

Zarga rubbed his scruffy chin. He thought about her suggestion a moment. "I need someone experienced to follow all these social justice protests." Zarga looked at her. "But I will take your recommendation to heart. We'll give her a try."

"Thanks Joe. Now what about this story?" Janine pointed to her typed pages on the desk.

"It's....it's just insane Janine. Vampire blood rituals and a massacre in a church? Sounds like something out of a horror film."

Janine reached over the desk and pointed her finger at him. "I'm telling you, this is all true. And I have the evidence. Joe, if you trust me, then go with the story. Publish. I'm telling you, on my life, this is ALL TRUE."

Zarga was silent. Janine sat back in her chair. "I'm asking you to trust me, Joe. One last time."

"I do trust you Janine. And that's what scares me. That this is....true." Zarga got up and started pacing around the office. He stopped at the window and looked down. "Millions of people in the city and vampires living among them. It's terrifying." He turned to face Janine. "We will publish the story. I have some minor edits, but not much. I'll give you double the stringer's fee. Front page, above the fold. Whatever you wish."

Janine smiled. "Thanks Joe."

"Now when can I see the evidence?"

"Meet me this afternoon, at 2. Coroner's office."

"Coroner's office?"

"You heard me."

"Sounds scarier than hell."

Janine got up and went to the office door. "See you at 2. You'll have your evidence." Janine opened the door to walk out.

"Janine." Zarga stopped her.

"Yes?"

"Since we are publishing the story....you mind telling me who the anonymous source was?"

Janine was hesitant to answer. She'd protected Painter every step of the way. He was dead now, and she certainly didn't need to keep on protecting him. He'd said that it would be okay to reveal his name if the story ever came to a conclusion. Now, it certainly had.

"You know what Joe. If I ever get brought into court over this, maybe I'll just have to tell you. Until then, I'd rather not answer that question." She gave him a hard stare, daring him to back down. After a moment, he did.

"Okay, Janine. Be careful. And great job."

Janine smiled at Zarga and walked out.

***

The newsroom was empty. Erica was out covering a story and so was Grossman. No one was there to say goodbye to her. It made Janine happy that she wouldn't have to have an emotional goodbye. She was sure she'd get calls and e-mails, maybe a thank you from Bev for recommending her for the job. She was happy that Bev would get a chance to prove herself.

Janine went to her desk and looked through all the drawers. She threw her reporter's notebooks into her backpack. She took a few pens and some sticky pads. She also made sure she had a copy of every number in her rolodex, just in case she'd ever need it down the road. She left the rolodex behind, so Bev would have easy access to a treasure trove of New York City sources and story ideas.

Janine took a final stroll through the newsroom and walked to the elevator. After waiting a moment for it to arrive, she decided to take the stairs instead. She walked down three floors and pushed the exit door. She crossed through the lobby. Her final voyage through the New York Daily Reporter offices.

On the street, it was a sunny day. The city was getting warmer, and hopefully the virus would be kept under better control because of it. That's what the doctors and the President seemed to think. She wasn't sure. She did know that there was one thing she'd never have to worry about finding her in sunlight--vampires. She smiled and started her walk to the subway.

A block away, Janine noticed a protest going on. There were about 40 people marching down the street, most in masks. Some were carrying signs. She heard one woman shout "No justice, no peace! No racist police!" Janine decided to follow them. She walked with them for two blocks until the group had reached a city park. In the park, a larger number of people had gathered in protest, listening to a speaker. There were a few cops nearby, who didn't seem happy to be there. They weren't doing anything to stop the protest. She also wasn't sure why the city didn't stop this many people from gathering together. This didn't seem to go in line with the city's policies on social distancing. Not everyone had a mask on, either.

Janine listened as the speaker shouted to the crowd. It was a social justice protest, advocating for police reform and better race relation policies. Janine listened for a few moments and stepped away to get home. Something however, was keeping her there, she realized. She looked around and couldn't see any reporters that she knew. No one from the Daily Reporter was there. Janine took out a reporter's notebook and a pen from her bag. She walked over to one of the protestors, a young black woman who was carrying a sign that said "Justice for George."

"I'm Janine Gomes, reporter," she said to the girl. "Writing a story today. Mind if I ask you a few questions?"

"Go ahead," the girl said.

"So why did you decide to come out today?"

The girl answered the question. Janine took notes and asked some follow-ups. Her first story as a freelancer. Of course, she would give Joe the first chance to run it. She was certain that he would.

Janine spent the next 20 minutes listening to the speakers and interviewing a few more people. She closed her notebook, and placed it and the pen back into her bag. Time to get to writing, she said to herself. Maybe it wouldn't be as easy as she thought to take a break from journalism. She smiled and started walking toward the train.

There in the crowd was the tiny figure. Janine couldn't see her, but she was there listening to it all and waiting. Dressed in black. Wearing large spectacles that reflected the sunlight. Hidden by the towering figures around her. She saw Janine's every move, observing it all quietly. When Janine finally walked away, the strega waited a moment before she started following her. Always behind by about 12 feet. Unobserved. Walking and walking, the sunlight shining brightly on her grey hair. A beautiful spring day.

ACKNOWLEDGMENTS

Thank you for reading my book. It took a lot of time and effort and I'm so grateful that out of all the millions of books you could have just read, you chose mine.

I want to thank my wife Jessica first and foremost, for all of her love and support through this entire process. She was a great editor and gave me plenty of really good ideas for the book.

Thank you so much to Krysti Dahlgren for designing the cover of the book.

Thank you to my family and friends for their constant love and support in the most difficult of times.

Made in the USA
Middletown, DE
04 October 2020